The
VOYAGE
of
LUCY P. SIMMONS

The
VOYAGE
of
LUCY P. SIMMONS

BARBARA MARICONDA

KATHERINE TEGEN BOOKS
An Imprint of HarperCollins Publishers

Katherine Tegen Books is an imprint of HarperCollins Publishers.

The Voyage of Lucy P. Simmons
Copyright © 2012 by Barbara Mariconda
All rights reserved. Printed in the United States of America.
No part of this book may be used or reproduced in any manner
whatsoever without written permission except in the case of
brief quotations embodied in critical articles and reviews.
For information address HarperCollins Children's Books,
a division of HarperCollins Publishers, 10 East 53rd Street,
New York, NY 10022. www.harpercollinschildrens.com

Library of Congress Cataloging-in-Publication Data is available.
ISBN 978-0-06-211979-7

Typography by Amy Ryan
12 13 14 15 16   LP/RRDH   10 9 8 7 6 5 4 3 2 1
❖
First Edition

For Pamela Bramhall,
who has journeyed with Lucy
from the very beginning.

The

VOYAGE

of

LUCY P. SIMMONS

1

COASTAL MAINE, 1906

There it was again—the sound of the ship's bell. Though there was no ship, and no wind, it clanged, echoing across the rocks and out over Simmons Point.

Addie stepped through the front door onto the veranda, where I sat snuggled in one of the oak rockers facing out to sea. Buried in my book, I hummed a scrap of the old sea chantey Father had taught me. *"A la dee dah dah, a la dee dah dee . . ."*

"There 'tis—that accursed bell," Addie exclaimed, pointing to the large brass toller Father had mounted against the wall beside the door.

"Ringin' of its own accord! Gives me the willies, I tell ye!"

She set a wicker picnic basket down beside the step. "If ye ask me, Miss Lucy, it's too early in the season fer a boat ride, but who'm I to question the cap'n?"

A boat ride? *And* a picnic! I threw the crocheted blanket from my lap, dropped my copy of *Treasure Island* onto the chair, gathered my skirts, and bounded down the steps.

"Won't be much of a picnic if ye leave behind the tea sandwiches," Addie called.

I turned, grabbed the basket, and took off across the lawn.

"Your shawl, missy! You'll need a shawl out there on the water! And one fer your mother as well!"

It was early April—the time of year when the coast of Maine is still mostly gray and brown, when a damp chill wraps itself around you and you think spring may never really come. But I pretended not to hear, the basket bumping heavily against my leg as I ran.

When I approached the garden, I slowed, out of breath and panting. Mother was tending her roses, clearing out the leaves that had cushioned them from the winter wind. When she saw me, she smiled, removed her apron, and hung it on the garden-shed hook. "I see Miss Addie told you Father's surprise!"

"We're going for a sail! Has Father already got the sloop in the water? Are we going all the way to Wiscasset? Can we—"

"Slow down, Lucille," Mother said gently, adjusting her wide-brimmed hat. "Father has a plan, I'm sure. All we need to do is walk—*walk*—down to the slip." She tweaked my chin and tousled my hair. "Here, darling, let me carry the basket; it's bigger than you are."

In no time we wove our way along the pine-edged path, across the craggy rocks, and down the hill to the place where Father tied the small sailboat.

"There they are," he boomed, "my two best girls!"

He bowed, gesturing toward his shipshape little sloop, which bobbed against the small dock. Mother smiled with just one side of her mouth and winked, like she did whenever he teased. In a grand sweep, he took the basket, placed it on board, then wrapped his arms around her. I wiggled in between them, hating the hint of that left-out feeling that tugged at me whenever they were close like that. But, as always, they pulled me into their little circle. Mother kissed the top of my head, and

Father squeezed me in a crushing hug.

And then, again, the ship's bell back at the house tolled.

We climbed aboard and settled in. Father untied the sloop and we pushed away. With a practiced hand he deftly worked the lines, raising its sails, and in minutes the light wind was spiriting us along. Mother pulled me close and wrapped us both in a thick wool blanket, then turned back the red-and-white checked cloth Addie had used to wrap our luncheon. "Chicken salad!" I exclaimed. "My favorite!" I popped one, then another small triangle into my mouth. "Hmmm," I said as I reached for a third.

"Slow down, sweet one," Mother said.

"No! Eat hearty!" Father exclaimed, smiling as he swallowed his fourth petite pointy sandwich. "Out on the water a sailor needs sustenance!"

"Oh, Edward," Mother said, tsking her tongue, "the things you teach her!"

"Oh, indeed! Lucy, shall we show Mother what else you've learned?" From his pocket he pulled a small flute of whalebone and hardwood, with nautical scenes carved around the finger holes. Years ago Father had crafted it aboard his ship, passing many a lonely evening. As the son of a seafaring family, he knew many chanteys from days of old. And now, so did I. He blew a cascade of notes, and I began:

We'll back up our topsails and heave our vessel to,
Blow high! Blow low! And so sailed we.
For we have got some letters to be carried home
*   by you,*
A-sailing down all on the coasts of High Barbaree.

For broadside! For broadside! the saucy pirates
*   cried—*

Here I stood and raised a fist as I sang out,

Blow high! Blow low! And so sailed we.
The broadside that we showed them was to sink
*   them in the tide!*
A-sailing down all on the coasts of High Barbaree.

Mother gasped. "Sit down, Lucille! You'll lose your footing!" But Father grinned, then blew the lilting melody with even more vigor. I waved my imaginary sword.

With cutlass and gun, oh, we fought for hours
*   three.*
Blow high! Blow low! And so sailed we.

The ship it was their coffin, and their grave it was the sea!
A-sailing down all on the coasts of High Barbaree.

Then he ended with the other tune, the one so old the words had been forgotten except for a snippet of the refrain. *"A la dee dah dah, a la dee dah dee,"* I hummed along on the wordless verses, then, as always, sang out on the *la dee dah dee*s. Father blew the last plaintive note, tucked the flute back into his pocket, and applauded. A frown had crept across Mother's face as she gazed across the water. "I don't like those songs," she said softly. "They remind me too much of your days at sea, Edward."

It was at that very moment that the fog began to roll in, eerily, ghostlike, swirling around our little sloop in long, misty wisps. In minutes the blue sky paled, and the sky, fog, and water became one seamless, white sheet.

Father stood very still, staring off through his spyglass with one squinted eye.

Mother shifted in her seat, her body tense and her brow knitted. "Edward," she called, "let's turn back. I can barely make out the shore from the open sea."

Father made a show of handing me his spyglass and flashed her a smile.

"It's but a fog coming in with the warmer air. Typical April in Maine, my dear. The shore's right there behind us. See the pines above the vapor?"

I hung the spyglass securely around my neck, then lifted it and peered through the lens. "Look, Mother," I said. "Not only can you see the tips of the pines—you can see the roof of our house!"

She squinted, a doubtful expression on her face.

"I'll bring her around, Johanna," Father said, and with a few polished moves he adjusted the sail so that it caught the slight breeze.

"All right, mates," he said lightly, "your job is to keep our castle in your sights while I take us in!"

He winked at me, and I glanced back toward our landmark. But the slate-covered turrets, and even the tops of the pines, had disappeared into the mist. Father followed my gaze, and a hint of a shadow crossed his face. Mother bit her bottom lip.

"We'll be fine, Mother," I said. After all, I reasoned, Father, a retired sea captain, had sailed huge ships across the open Atlantic. What was a little fog along the shore next to the storms he'd faced at sea?

Father turned and cocked his head.

"What is it, Edward?" Mother asked.

"Sh!" Father said. "I believe I hear a distress call. . . ."

"But Edward!" Mother's voice had a frantic edge. The sky was growing darker, an odd pea-green tinge to it, giving the water a threatening, steel-gray cast. The wind picked up, ruffling the ribbon on Mother's hat and turning back the brim.

"Hold this line, Johanna," Father said, handing her a coil of rope. "Just keep the boat steady."

Mother held the rope with white knuckles.

"I'll help," I whispered, wrapping my hands around hers, as much to feel her close to me as to help steady the sloop, which had begun to pitch back and forth with the rising waves.

Father took us farther out, straining his eyes and leaning into the wind.

"What in the world?" he said, almost to himself.

That's when I heard—faintly—a man's voice calling out. In seconds it was swallowed up by the whoosh of a cresting wave. I heard it again, along with a yipping, howling sound.

"Edward," my mother called, "turn around, please. It's getting rough!"

"I hear someone calling for help," Father said. "We can't very well ignore him."

"Help! Somebody help me!"

The first drops of rain pelted down in large, cold splats.

"For the love of God," Father said softly. "Look over there."

At first all that was visible was the outline of a small, dilapidated rowboat.

"Ahoy there," Father called. "We're coming around."

"Help me, for God's sake!" yelled the voice. "I'm sinking!"

"Stay calm, man," Father called. "We're coming."

The water grew rough and I gripped the sides of the boat. Father maneuvered expertly, and in no time we were alongside the rowboat, which was rapidly taking on water.

A huge bear of a man was waving his arms, his ragged black beard and shoulder-length hair blowing about wildly. There was a large gash on his forehead. Blood streamed down his cheek and onto his dirty shirt. A small, tawny dog with a pushed-in face and curly tail jumped about, barking frantically.

"Shut up, you flea-bitten mongrel," the man yelled, kicking the unfortunate beast with his filthy black boots.

"Oh, good Lord, what a brute," gasped Mother.

"It's all right, Johanna," Father whispered. "We'll only need to have him aboard for a short while." He threw a heavy line over to the man's boat.

"Grab hold, and pull us in closer."

The man reached, stumbled, and fell forward. His boat dipped and bobbed precariously. Mother screamed, and the little dog began jumping and yapping all over again.

Father threw our life preserver toward the man. "Calm down and use the life buoy!" he shouted. The man stood unsteadily and, instead of grabbing the ring, flung himself toward us, overturning his boat. Both man and dog tumbled into the sea.

"Jesus H. Christ!"

I knew Father was concerned, for he never used the Lord's name in vain. The brute splashed toward our boat and gripped the side. Mother and I screamed as our sloop lurched dangerously. Father, now lying on his belly, grabbed the man and pulled. A huge wave splashed over them, dragging the man under. He emerged, terrified, and broke from Father's grasp.

"Don't panic," Father yelled. "Just take my hand!"

The man disappeared underwater again. This time he didn't resurface. Only the dog was visible, paddling strenuously around the capsized boat. "No, Father!" I screamed, as he peeled off his topcoat.

"Edward, no!" Mother stood, reaching out for him, the boat rocking wildly.

"I can't let the man drown!" Father yelled. "Johanna, just hold tight to that line!"

With that, Father dived into the sea.

"Oh God, oh my dear God!" Mother whispered, over and over again.

My eyes darted about, trying to fix Father in my sights. I saw him break the surface, gasping for air, his dark hair slick to his head. He had the man's massive arm draped about his shoulders and he swam in a frog-like crawl back toward our boat.

"Freezing," Mother whispered. "Dear God, Edward, you must be freezing!"

Finally, Father was at the edge of the stern. The dog paddled vigorously alongside them, his head bobbing just above the water. Mother reached over, still grasping the line. "Edward, darling, grab my hand," she shouted.

Their hands touched, and for a moment I thought everything would be all right. But as Mother bent over, the brute grabbed the line. I saw it all in slow motion—the way the thick rope looked small in his massive hands as he yanked it toward him, the look of horror on Father's face as Mother toppled over the side, the crazy angle of her body hitting the water, her skirts billowing out around her, her broad-brimmed hat disappearing in the dark-gray sea.

"Mother!" I screamed.

"I'll get her, Lucy," Father shouted.

I watched him struggle to free himself from the brute's desperate grasp. A great flash of lightning ripped the sky in two. I screamed when I heard the whack of Father's head against the side of our boat.

I don't know why I jumped into the water. I only knew that that was where Mother and Father were.

It was so much colder than I ever dreamed, my skirts wrapping around me like icy fingers. I thrashed about, fighting the waves, which seemed intent on pulling me under. The salt stung my eyes and burned my nose, and despite how much I willed it to be so, I could neither see my parents nor stay afloat.

The last thing I remembered was the bottom of the boat swinging around toward me, and the dull thud as it hit me square in the forehead. For a moment the sky swirled madly above me, and finally even the sky was swallowed up by the icy, gray nothingness of the angry sea.

2

The feeling of being thrown about in the waves like a rag doll, gulping and choking on salt water was so vivid, and the terror of the underwater darkness so real, that it was some time before I realized that I was no longer, in fact, still there in the sea. It was that strange yipping, insistent and urgent, that seemed to draw me out of the darkness.

Slowly, slowly, I came to, gradually realizing that the tangle of cloth around my arms and legs was no longer my cold, wet skirts, but something dry and warm. Opening my eyes seemed an impossible task, so heavy were my eyelids. It took a great effort to open them, fighting to keep my eyes from rolling back in my head.

It was dark, but not the cold, inky blackness of the sea. A warm, soft darkness greeted me, and recognition melted over me like a salve. It was my very own room I lay in; the tangle of cloth around me, my very own bedclothes!

With difficulty I hoisted myself up on my elbows. I blinked in the dark, fighting the throbbing in my head.

It had been a dream then, after all—a terrible, bad dream! I closed my eyes to the memory of it, wincing at the images that crept into my brain. Mother, and then Father . . .

No . . . no. . . . I squeezed my eyes shut and shook my head. I was home in my own bed, safe in our own house. The house creaked as if to reassure me, a familiar sound I'd never appreciated before.

But that other sound . . . that yipping. There was something familiar about it, too. I forced my eyes open again and turned toward the noise. At first, what appeared before me was a kaleidoscope of muted shapes and colors. I squinted harder and rubbed at my eyes. Slowly the jumbled images converged, and my eyes crossed in an effort to bring the scene before me into focus.

A sound escaped my lips as I saw clearly for

the first time. It was a little dog. A small, tawny dog with a blackish, pushed-in face; short, bowed legs; and a tail curled up like a pig's. I fell back on the pillow and tried to control the racing of my heart. It was the dream again . . . the boat, the brutish man and his dog. How in the world could the pathetic pup be here in my room? My lips and mouth felt suddenly parched, and the room spun. Maybe I was delirious. Hallucinating. Perhaps I had lost my mind, maybe in the stupor of a fever.

But the yipping was real enough, although softer now. I closed my eyes and heard a rapid clicking noise. I realized it was the retreat of the animal, the sound of its little nails tapping along Mother's polished wooden floors. Mother wouldn't like that, not one bit.

But then, the clicking returned, followed by the sound of footsteps. I felt a cool hand on my forehead.

I looked up to find Addie, her white apron tied over her crisp blue dress.

"Oh, lass," she whispered, stroking my face, the hint of her Irish brogue creeping into her voice as it did whenever she was excited. "There ye' are, finally." She turned and hurried toward the door.

"Mrs. Simmons," she called, her voice urgent, "'tis time to come up here, 'tis! Miss Lucy is awake!

Do come quickly!"

Her words caused a quake in the pit of my stomach. She was calling to Mother! A small smile spread across my face, and the tension I'd felt began to melt away. I was home safe in my bed, and Mother was coming to me. I closed my eyes, saving my strength for the sight of her.

I heard her feet on the stairs, heavy and fast, so unlike Mother's usual dainty, graceful step. She was worried, of course, I reasoned, and thinking of nothing but of getting to me more quickly.

In seconds I felt her take my hand. I opened my eyes slowly, anticipating how I would drink in the sight of her.

First, the kaleidoscope, a great dark splotch spinning round before my eyes. I shook my head slightly and scrunched my eyes very hard, peering out beneath lowered brows.

I blinked several times and sat up as best I could. The image before me came into focus. I froze.

The woman holding my hand wasn't my mother at all, but a complete stranger! She was making soft clicking noises with her tongue.

"There, there, now," she said. "There, there."

I stared at her for a moment. She was a short, plump woman, with full cheeks and small, close-set blue eyes. She had thin lips and several chins beneath the first one, which sat like a miniature apple beneath her mouth.

I looked past her toward the door.

"Where's Mother?" I asked, my voice not much more than a raspy cackle.

The plump woman squeezed my hand and opened and closed her mouth several times. She glanced at Addie.

"Oh goodness," she said, finally. "She doesn't remember. Perhaps it's a blessing."

"Mother!" I yelled, this time much louder. The word seemed to stick in my mouth, and my throat began to tighten. "Mother! Where's Mother?" I croaked. "Addie, I heard you call for her." I yanked my hand away from the woman. The small dog began to whimper and turn his head this way and that.

"Oh, dear," said the woman, shaking her head. "You'd better tell her, Miss Addie. I can't do it. I just don't have it in me."

Addie came around and sat on the side of my bed. She took a deep breath and wiped her hands on her apron.

"Lucy," she said quietly, "'twas an accident out on the water, there was. A terrible accident."

"No," I said, covering my ears and shaking my head. "No! I'm not listening to you!" I was angry at her then, and angrier still at the plump woman, who was dabbing at her eyes with a hankie.

Though I wouldn't look at her, Addie continued. I stuffed my fingers in my ears and shut my eyes tight, but, try as I might, I couldn't shut her out.

"I know how difficult 'tis for ye, Lucy, an' how awful it must be to remember. But your mother and the captain were drowned out there on the water. A hero, your father was, in the saving of another. The odd fellow was seen floatin' ashore grasping the edge of yer little sloop, he was." She paused as tears slipped beneath my crunched lids.

"'Twas a miracle you survived a'tall," she said softly, "but thanks t' the life preserver, the wee pup Mr. Pugsley here, and the help of a stranger who witnessed the scene, ye were dragged, 'bout nearly lifeless, out of the water to shore, yer father's spyglass hangin' round yer neck. And even then, what with the water in your lungs and the pneumonia, we thought for a bit we might lose ye as well. Thank goodness you've come out of it, finally. Your auntie here and your uncle have been waitin'. They'll be here to care for ye, they will. 'Twill be better, in time, you'll see."

Addie's voice cracked a little, and she put her arms around me. As much as I wanted someone to hold me, hers were not the arms I needed. I pushed her away, collapsed into my pillows, and turned my face from them. I felt the dog leap onto the bed, felt his snuffling nose against my face. I yanked the bedclothes over my head and remained that way until I heard them all—all except for the dog, that is—retreat into the hallway, talking in whispers.

And that was how I came to meet my father's sister-in-law, my aunt Margaret, and the boat-wreck dog, Mr. Pugsley, and how I came to understand that bad dreams, terrible dreams, can sometimes be all too real.

3

It was my uncle Victor, ultimately, who saw to it that I recovered in short time—that I was up and about and able to at least make a *show* of being well. Now, you're probably thinking that I was quite fortunate to have had someone coaxing me back to health—someone relentlessly pushing me on along the road to recovery.

But I was neither fortunate nor lucky. In fact, my uncle Victor was scarcely concerned for anything but the reading of Mother and Father's will—an event that our old friend and attorney Barrister Hardy insisted take place in my presence and, as he put it, with me healthy again in both body and spirit.

Judging from what little I knew of my father's younger brother (Father had alluded to Uncle Victor's financial woes and hinted at a certain chronic lack of determination on his brother's part), it may well have been that pressing, for my recuperation had been his greatest accomplishment to date.

My heart ached as we gathered in the library for the reading of the will—Aunt Margaret, Uncle Victor, Barrister Hardy, and me. And of course, my new companion, Mr. Pugsley, sitting watch at my feet. The barrister was seated at Father's desk; the rest of us sat facing him on the oak folding chairs from the game room—the very same ones we used to use for an evening of keno or chess. Ghostly memories of Mother and Father in happier days surrounded me here, making the task at hand nearly unbearable.

Barrister Hardy, a very proper Englishman who was always shy and bookish, seemed particularly uncomfortable, adjusting his small round spectacles and shuffling and reshuffling the stack of papers before him. He sent for Addie, requesting her presence as a witness to the proceedings. She came, rather grim-faced, wiping her hands on her apron as though preparing for some loathsome household task. She draped an arm around me, but it provided little comfort.

The barrister cleared his throat. "As you all know, we are here today for the reading of the last will and testament of Edward R. and Johanna E. Simmons." He glanced up at us briefly and looked back at his papers. I watched my uncle, his eyes gleaming, leaning forward in his chair. He patted my hand in what I supposed was meant to be a gesture of sympathy. It was all I could do not to pull my hand away, for the hungry look in his eye told another story. Aunt Margaret twisted a hankie round and round her chubby fingers, glancing nervously back and forth between her husband and the barrister.

Barrister Hardy sat up a bit straighter and began to read.

"'I, Edward R. Simmons, being of sound mind and memory, do hereby make, publish, and declare this to be my last will and testament, expressly revoking all wills heretofore made by me and declare this will to remain in effect . . .'"

The words droned on—Father's words, I suppose—words I hardly understood, phrases that sounded stiff and cold and wooden to my ear.

Uncle Victor edged forward in his chair, licking

his thin lips, hungrily devouring and digesting each word.

"'I give, devise, and bequeath my estate of whatever nature and wherever situated to my sister, Miss Prudence Faith Simmons, in trust for my daughter, Lucille Prudence Simmons. . . .'"

Aunt Margaret's hand went to her mouth, her small eyes open wide. Uncle Victor opened and shut his mouth several times. That, combined with his slicked-back hair, gave him the look of a slippery seal begging for a fish. He jumped to his feet, sending Mr. Pugsley into a new round of yipping.

"Now, wait just a minute," Victor began.

Barrister Hardy raised a hand, silencing him. He had the same effect on Mr. Pugsley, who plopped back down at my feet with an impatient sort of *hmpff.* I looked between them, feeling rather lost. Aunt Prudence, my father's sister, hadn't been heard from in quite some time. She was an eccentric woman—casting aside afternoons of high tea and croquet on the lawn for free-spirited world traveling.

Uncle Victor sat down, and Barrister Hardy went on. "'Miss Simmons will oversee the estate until my daughter Lucille attains the age of eighteen. Furthermore, I hereby nominate and appoint Prudence Faith Simmons as guardian of my daughter Lucille, as she may be a minor. In the event that said shall die, resign, or be unwilling or unable to act as guardian, then I hereby declare that Barrister Franklin P. Hardy nominate and appoint an appropriate substitute. Additionally, our trusted friend Miss Addelaide Clancy will remain in our employ as live-in nanny and housekeeper, overseeing Lucille's day-to-day needs. A generous trust has been established for this purpose. I also request that Miss Clancy remain in residence until Lucille's eighteenth birthday, and thereafter as long as Lucille deems necessary.'"

The barrister paused.

"What does that mean?" I asked.

"It means hogwash!" Uncle Victor shouted. "Absolute hogwash. It is obvious that Edward was not of sound mind when he appointed *Prudence* to be in charge! She is unstable and reckless. She doesn't know her place. She is hardly a decent role model for the girl! I am the man's brother, and my wife and I can—"

"Just a minute," said Barrister Hardy. "Wait just one minute."

He turned to me. "Lucy, what this means is that your mother and father requested that, in the event of their deaths, your aunt Prudence would come here to take care of you. She would take care of their estate—in other words, their money—until you are old enough to take care of it yourself. Miss Addie will remain on the payroll to look after you and the house as she has always done."

"This is outrageous!" bellowed Victor. Aunt Margaret reached toward him.

"But Victor, why don't you—"

"You stay out of this, Margaret," he shouted. "You'd do best to keep your nose out of affairs you cannot possibly understand."

She pulled her hand away and sniffed a little. "But Vic—"

"Quiet!" he snapped. "Now, I demand that—"

"There will be no demands honored here except those laid out by your brother," the barrister said stiffly. "This document in my hands is legal and binding. I can assure you that Edward was in sound mind when it was drawn up. Now, if you would be so kind as to let me finish, I think you might hear what you obviously were so hoping to hear."

My heart sank at those words. I couldn't imagine that anything Uncle Victor would like to hear would be in my best interest.

"So," I asked, "what about Aunt Prudence?" I didn't know my aunt well, but had loved the tales of her adventures, loved the photographs of her with her long, wild, curly hair, so like my own. "When will she come?"

Barrister Hardy sighed. "That is precisely the problem. My office has been trying to locate your aunt since we received the news of your parents' untimely deaths. She was last reported to be in Australia, in the outback country. She was working with an archaeologist, exploring aboriginal caves, on a quest of some sort. Despite our best efforts, we could not reach her. We can only hope that at some point she will make an effort to contact her brother. At this time she is unaware of the situation here."

"She could be *dead* for all we know," shouted Victor, once again jumping to his feet.

"Oh, good Lord," muttered Addie, who up to this point had remained silent. "Miss Prudence is most certainly not dead!"

Victor's face was red, his nostrils flared.

"May I remind you, missy," said Victor, through clenched teeth, "that you are a servant here. A *servant*, do you hear me? Your job is to be seen and not heard!"

"Another of my brother's faults," he said to the barrister, jutting out his chin toward Addie, "allowing the help to behave as though they were on equal footing. That, and entrusting his child to our dreamer of a sister. Is it any wonder someone with so little judgment would endanger the lives of his wife and child in order to save a drunkard on a boat? It's a wonder anyone is surprised at all by this sad state of affairs!"

I felt as though I'd been slapped. I gasped, and Addie knelt beside me, rubbing my hand. "Don't pay him any mind," she whispered. "Don't listen to him a'tall!" But I did pay him mind—I hated him then, and nearly hated my aunt Prudence as well, for her absence, and Mother and Father for theirs. They'd left me, all of them, left me entirely alone with this horrid uncle and his wife. Thank goodness I'd still have Addie. Dear, sweet, loyal Addie.

Barrister Hardy turned very red, a deep angry flush that began at his collar and crept up his face. "That will be enough!" he said. "Mr. Simmons, you will remain silent until I am finished."

Uncle Victor sat back down, in quite a huff. Barrister Hardy continued.

"It seems to me that, in the absence of any other family, I have no other choice but to appoint Victor T. and Margaret K. Simmons guardians of Lucille and overseers of the house and estate."

I watched Uncle Victor mouth the word *yes*, his eyes narrowed, the word escaping as a quiet hiss. At that very moment, as if in protest, the shutters on the library window inexplicably blew shut with a bang, knocking one of Father's seascapes off the wall. The sound made all of us jump, particularly because we hadn't been aware of any wind. The gust also took up Father's ship's bell out by the front door. It clanged loudly, eerily, as if sounding a death knell or perhaps announcing the launching of a phantom ship. Looking back, I recollect this clearly, because it was the first real hint about the house, the first indication that there was indeed something very strange about to take place. But at the time I didn't pay much attention. My mind was still reeling at the prospect of having Uncle Victor and Aunt Margaret as my guardians.

Uncle Victor thrust the painting haphazardly back onto the wall, the scene of Ulysses and his crew tipped like a sinking ship. He went on to the window and attempted to push the shutters back, but it seemed as though they suddenly had a mind of their own, and they continued to defy him. He pushed and grimaced and struggled with the shutters until Addie came over to help. She reached out and took hold of the shutters, which moved easily under her gentle touch, mocking my uncle's efforts. This infuriated him further.

"I don't remember asking for your help, missy," he said. He turned back toward the barrister. "Now, let's get on with it!"

"As I said," Barrister Hardy continued, in a chilly tone of voice, "until Miss Prudence can be found, Mr. Simmons, you and your wife will serve as guardians. However, when Miss Prudence is located, guardianship will revert back to her, and your responsibilities here will be complete."

"And if she isn't found?" asked Uncle Victor.

"Then you remain guardians for the next six years, until Lucy turns eighteen. And Miss Clancy, do you agree to stay on as stipulated in Captain Simmons's last will and testament?"

Addie grabbed my hand. "Yes, of course, Barrister. I wouldn't think a leavin'."

Uncle Victor silenced her with a wave of his hand.

"Another question—I must ask, however awkward," he began. His tone of voice was suddenly very different—syrupy, artificially sweet. He glanced my way and back at the barrister.

"And what if, let's say, something should happen to Miss Lucy *before* her eighteenth birthday? I mean, after all, tragedies do occur, as we have recently witnessed." He looked around for encouragement. Aunt Margaret stared at her feet, blinking nervously.

"It is only responsible to ask," he continued, glancing from one to the other of us.

The question hung there like a bad omen. Aunt

Margaret stared at her shoes. Addie took a deep breath, bit her bottom lip, and seemed unable to move. My heart pounded, and for an instant I wished that the sea had taken me along with Mother and Father.

Barrister Hardy paused, removed his glasses, and rubbed his eyes.

"In the case of Miss Lucy's untimely death, the house and estate would revert to the legal guardian."

Uncle Victor smiled, a thin-lipped smile that had little warmth in it.

"Thank you, Barrister," he said. "One has to consider all of the possibilities, however unlikely."

I spoke up. "But, Barrister, why couldn't there be a different guardian—Miss Addie, even?"

Barrister Hardy tipped his head toward me and spoke gently. "I imagine Miss Addie would make a fine guardian. But this house that your father built is a continuation of the Simmonses' seafaring legacy. As I recall, he referred to it as his 'ship on shore.'" He glanced at Father's leather-bound ship's logs on the desk, the nautical treasures that lined the shelves and walls. "I know his intent was to keep the house, and everything in it—especially *you*, my dear—in the family's loving care."

I started to protest, but the barrister silenced

me with a firm, but sad, smile.

"The law upholds this last will and testament. No one could have anticipated the tragic circumstances we find ourselves in this day."

Uncle Victor looked triumphant.

And then and there, I knew that I was no longer going to be safe—and not only in the sense of being well loved and cared for. I shuddered to think beyond that, refused to consider what my uncle might have in store for me.

At that very moment, as if to lock away any further thoughts in that regard, the shutters made one more defiant slam against the window.

And, in answer, Father's ship's bell out front clanged its warning again—a sound as hollow and lonely as the feelings that had taken over my spirit in the days since the accident.

But the bell's warning was not lost on me. Despite my sadness, it awoke in me a level of resolve I had never before experienced—a determination that left a steely taste in my mouth, an energy and electricity in my soul that had been absent for some time.

It's not that I had any real inkling at all as to what I should do. In fact, I hadn't a single notion.

Nevertheless, I set my jaw and raised my chin in a silent vow that I made not only to myself, but to

Mother and Father as well—that I, Lucy P. Simmons, would *do* something. Something to save my home—our home—Father's ship on shore. Something to keep it safe from my uncle's greedy hands.

I only had to figure out what in heaven's name it was I ought to do.

4

The plan came to me that evening—after midnight, it had to have been. I had slept fitfully, tossing and turning through the early evening hours, wrestling with my bedclothes as well as with the problems at hand.

The answer was, of course, to find Aunt Prudence. The question was, how to go about it. I forced myself to lie still, to calm my mind, which was reeling about, relentlessly replaying the events of the day.

What did I know of my aunt, of Father's younger sister, Prudence? She'd visited here at the house, some years ago now, it seemed. She was high-spirited, I recalled, and I remembered being enraptured by her bold ideas and her tales of travel. She and Mother were very close, and in between visits I would watch Mother standing by the library desk, the sterling silver letter opener in her hand, eagerly slicing open her sister-in-law's letters from wherever in the world she'd been.

It was that image of Mother enthusiastically reading Aunt Pru's correspondence that gave me the notion. Why hadn't I thought of it sooner? Of the stack of letters, tied neatly with a red satin ribbon, that Mother kept in the bottom drawer of Father's desk? There might lie the key to my aunt Pru's whereabouts!

I pushed the snoring Mr. Pugsley off of my legs and slipped out of bed. I grabbed my shawl from the chair, lit the small kerosene lantern on my nightstand, and tiptoed into the hallway, lamp in hand. I carefully lowered the wick so that all the lamp gave off was enough of a glow to just light my way. I walked noiselessly, with a stealth I hadn't known I was capable of. I couldn't risk waking Uncle Victor or Aunt Margaret, didn't want to arouse their attention. I scarcely breathed as I silently set first one foot, and then the other, on the stairs past their chamber. The staircase suddenly seemed my ally, for not one board let out a groan, not one plank so much as a creak. I slunk among the shadows, blending into the darkness as though the house and I were one.

I swept into the library like a ghost, leaving the door ajar so as to hear any movement from the upper floor. I practically floated over toward the desk and gently set down the lamp.

The desk seemed just as Father had left it. I stood for a moment, imagining his hands on the drawer pulls, the graceful fountain pen in his hand. I swallowed hard as I took Mother's silver letter opener and slid it into the pocket of my dressing gown. This was something that should be mine. I wouldn't risk having it fall into my aunt's chubby fingers, nor my uncle's greedy grasp.

I fell to my knees and pulled the drawer—the lower right drawer—ever so gently. A familiar dark, woody aroma escaped as it opened. I inhaled deeply and reached my hopeful hands inside.

My heart was fairly racing. I felt the bundle immediately—the fine, dry envelopes; the tiny jagged edges of the postage stamps in the corners; the smooth, cool satin ribbon that held, I prayed, the secrets that I sought. I thought of poring over the correspondence right then and there, crouched behind the desk, but it was a desire I thought best to curb. It simply wasn't worth the risk of being discovered. Instead I tucked the bundle into my pocket beside the letter opener, and pulled my shawl tightly around me.

As I stood to leave, my eye was drawn to the tall library windows. Each diamond-shaped pane seemed to sparkle in the moonlight. I could not ever remember being in the room at that hour, at a time of night when everything familiar seemed rather odd and cold in the dim light. I had intended to leave immediately, to return to my room as swiftly as I'd come, but I hesitated. Perhaps it was the light of the moon spilling into the room, or perhaps it was something else. The night felt peculiar, but I could not determine whether it felt menacing or magical, or whether perhaps the strangeness was just me, drowning in the feeling of being so completely alone.

I went to the window and stood, my mind as blank and as gray as a slate rubbed clean. The moon was full—a gigantic cool white pearl suspended over the ocean. I had never seen a moon quite like it before.

I stood, nearly hypnotized, staring out at the pale white moonbeams dancing across the black water, creating a shimmering path of light from horizon to shore.

Thinking I'd indulged myself long enough, I

started to turn from the window. But then I saw something.

It was only the smallest of movements out there that caught my eye and held me at the window. There was someone outside—someone on the path of the moonbeams. Not quite trusting my own eyes, I leaned forward, squinting. I rushed back to Father's desk and picked up the spyglass. At the window I extended the tubular lens and peered through it. The distant shore jumped into close view, requiring a second to reacclimate myself to this new perspective.

It was a woman. She swam in long, graceful strokes, barely rippling the water around her. I watched as she pulled herself from the sea and shook herself off. She tossed back her head, her long silver hair swinging away from her face in a brilliant, sleek sheet that sent a shower of water droplets in an arc behind her.

A wave of foolish disappointment washed over me. I had thought—or desperately hoped—that somehow the woman in the water was Mother. But of course, it wasn't. How could it be?

Despite my disappointment, there was a feeling of strength about her that pulled at me, as if a brush with her might transfer a measure of her fortitude my way.

I watched her wrap a large pale blanket around her narrow frame. Then she turned and stared up in my direction, toward the house. It was not a casual gaze—not at all—rather, it was focused and intense. I drew back from the window and into the shadows, still watching, hopefully undetected.

The old woman knelt at the water's edge and scooped up a handful of the sea. I stared, fascinated, as she lifted her chin up toward the house, shut her eyes, and placed her cupped palm just beneath her lips. She inhaled deeply and blew at the water in her hand, much the way Mother would blow a cascade of feather-light bath bubbles as we soaked in the tub. Or perhaps it was a kiss, blown my way.

A noise in the hallway broke my reverie. I spun from the window and listened so intently that my entire face hurt. It was a soft and rhythmic clicking sound approaching along the stairway.

It was Mr. Pugsley, of course. I rushed to the door and scooped his wriggling body up in my arms. I prayed he would remain quiet, and fought the urge to cover his small black muzzle with my hand. I stood perfectly still, struggling to detect any sound whatever, straining until the silence itself seemed thunderous in my ears.

Satisfied that Mr. Pugsley and I were the only ones awake, I shifted my attention back to the window. I held Mr. Pugsley firmly, his stocky little body neatly tucked under my left arm. I reached again for the spyglass, this time anchoring it in place with only my right hand. I stared through the lens and gasped.

A brilliant mist seemed to float and gently cascade off the roof of our house, curling in wispy clouds around the bay of windows where I stood. I took the lens from my eye for a second and pushed the hinged glass panel all the way open, allowing the vapors to filter in. The room felt suddenly alive with energy, a tingle that was almost physical. Even Mr. Pugsley was enchanted, I was convinced—the way he lay within my grasp, calm as I'd ever seen him, and silent, with barely a trace of his usual wheezing and panting. I, too, felt unnaturally calm in such a peculiar circumstance. Once again I gazed through the lens, wondering if the old woman had noticed this strange phenomenon.

Through the lens I saw her watch the house, her lips parted slightly, eyebrows raised. But then, suddenly, she turned, as though startled. She backed up, her posture stiff, her face alert. I aimed my spyglass off in the direction in which she was peering.

I must say, I do not know how I was able to even hold the scope steady, so shocked was I at the sight before me. I must have stiffened, for Mr. Pugsley began to bristle and squirm, a growl rumbling in his small, broad chest.

The old woman continued to back up, her eyes never leaving the Brute, who appeared out of the pine grove before her. Yes, it was the Brute—the wild bear of a man who had been the cause of Mother and Father's accident. He lunged at the old woman, and my heart nearly stopped beating. I watched in a kind of suspended dread as the woman continued backing up, step by step, into the sea, the water rising around her ankles, then her knees. The Brute yelled something at her, his voice lost to me in the wind. He waved his arms wildly and approached the water's edge. But the old woman just continued her retreat, holding him on the shore with only her gaze, calmly and deliberately backing out farther and farther along the moonbeam path into the sea. She continued until all that was visible was a circular ripple on the surface where the water enveloped the top of her head, her silver hair streaming out for a moment and then disappearing from view. I stared, transfixed. Mr. Pugsley began to bark, that high-pitched yipping that had punctuated the boating nightmare that took my father and mother from me.

To my horror, the Brute cocked his head as if listening, and slowly turned, peering straight up at the house. I clamped my hand over the dog's muzzle and, in my struggle to silence him, somehow let the spyglass slip from my grasp. As it hit the floor, there was a harsh clank of metal followed by a sickening shattering of glass. I found that I could not move, could scarcely breathe for the beating of my heart.

And then a shuffling sound overhead. A shuffling sound and a voice—clearly my uncle's.

That, and then the sound of his approaching footsteps on the stairs.

5

Still hugging Mr. Pugsley, I stepped into the
nook between the edge of the tall bookcase
and the windowsill, inching back as much as I
could so as to move out of the moonlit area around
Father's desk.

With each approaching step I realized that, of
course, we would be discovered. As if the broken
spyglass wasn't enough to prove my guilt, there sat
the lamp glowing on the desktop, illuminating the
gaping lower drawer—not to mention the wide-
open window, curtains billowing like sails on
a ship. "Who's there?" he called from down the

corridor. "Who's there, I say?"

Mr. Pugsley squirmed and growled, and I held him close, praying he'd settle down. I thought of just answering, of making some excuse about not being able to sleep, but my tongue felt thick and my voice couldn't seem to connect with the breath to carry it. I stood dumb, silent, waiting to be found.

Uncle Victor approached the door. The soft glow of the lamp began to expand, and from it emanated a small swirl of the same glittering vapor I'd seen float through the window. Mr. Pugsley and I stared, hypnotized, our eyes following the vapor that was traveling like a graceful swarm of microscopic fireflies. The sparkling mist surrounded the lamp, snuffing out the flame, and then drifted over the desktop toward the drawer.

An instant before Uncle Victor stepped into the room, Mr. Pugsley and I watched, openmouthed and bug-eyed, as the mist silently ushered the desk drawer shut, and then drifted on along the moonbeam toward the window. The diamond-shaped panes were suddenly shrouded in the shimmering mist, a magical vaporous curtain that seemed to draw the window shut. At the same time, another sparkling cloud spread beneath the broken spyglass, buoying it up from the floor. This was accompanied by the barely audible tinkling sounds of shards of glass hovering alongside, reconverging in the open end of the spyglass.

The mist all but disappeared as Uncle Victor stepped into the room, and for an instant I wondered whether or not I'd actually seen it. But of course I'd seen it—how else could one explain the snuffed-out lamp, the snug drawer and windows, the spyglass all shipshape again in one piece? I retreated as far back into the shadows as I could, my hope of remaining undetected suddenly rekindled.

Uncle Victor moved toward the center of the room, slowly, warily, his head cocked to one side, eyes narrowed. I held my breath as he rounded the far side of the desk. If he were to glance over his shoulder into the path of the moonlight, he would surely glimpse Mr. Pugsley and me pressed up against the side of the bookcase.

This time I didn't actually see the vapor—but I felt it, surrounding the edge of the shelving from ceiling to floor. It was a light tingling sensation, like thousands of very fine pins and needles that pulsed between me and the shelf. As Uncle Victor peered in our direction, the most uncanny thing of all occurred. The edge of the bookcase began to breathe—at least that's the way it seemed to me. It was as though the very wood itself inhaled, puffing up and out, swelling and expanding just enough to block Uncle Victor's view of me, and mine of him.

He stood for a minute, silently. I could nearly feel his eyes hungrily taking in every detail of the room, searching, scanning, skimming for evidence of anything out of place. The moment hung there between us and I could practically feel the shelf around me holding its breath, waiting . . . waiting.

After what seemed like an eternity, my uncle Victor swore softly under his breath and retreated, his bedroom slippers making a hollow flapping noise along the floor.

I heard the diminishing sound of his footfalls on the stairs, the murmur of Aunt Margaret's voice, and the creak of the bed as he laid his narrow frame back down.

We stayed still, Mr. Pugsley and I, for what seemed like an eternity. Finally, Mr. Pugsley squirmed out of my arms, and I leaned over to let him down. I stepped out from the shadows and looked about.

Nothing was amiss, not a thing out of place. Mr. Pugsley walked this way and that, nose to the ground, sniffing the space around the desk, beneath the window. I tiptoed over to the desk and picked up Father's spyglass with trembling hands. It was completely intact, just as it had always been.

I turned toward the window and peered outside. An unearthly stillness hung over the place—even the water seemed flat and unusually calm. There was no sign of the old woman, no sign of the Brute. A dark cloud passed in front of the moon, a smoky silhouette veiling the luminous pearl. The moonbeam path slowly disappeared, handing the library back over to the night. In the darkness the whole episode suddenly seemed unreal to me, impossible.

Yet the pack of letters sat in my pocket against my hip, and I'd not been discovered.

I bent and picked Mr. Pugsley up, and took my lamp in my hand. As I moved toward the door, the room itself seemed to release a sound like a sigh—a very deep sigh, or a hushed whisper.

I turned back and paused for a moment.

"Thank you," I answered, but to whom or to what, I had no idea.

6

Back in my room, I laid my bedclothes along the bottom of the door to block even the smallest wink of lamplight from escaping into the hallway. The house was still, but I could not risk being discovered, should Uncle Victor be struggling with sleeplessness after the disturbance in the library.

I sat on the floor, my back against the door, ears attuned to any hint of movement in the house. My lamp flickered beside me as I, with trembling fingers, untied the bundle. The papers fell into my lap like thin, dry leaves. I slipped the first letter out of its envelope and unfolded the ivory sheets of parchment, revealing Aunt Pru's ornate, practiced script.

June 13, 1903
My Dearest Johanna,

    I do pray this letter finds you well and happy! And that your dear seaman continues to thrive on shore! I often, during the evening and around our campfire, imagine the three of you snug in that marvelous mansion of yours facing the wild Atlantic, enjoying the quiet life of art and leisure you so desired!

    I continually marvel at how the two of us could be so different and still love each other so! And, sadly, it vexes me that my dear brother continues to deny the validity of my quest. I can say, with some certainty, that I have uncovered important clues to our family's past—on the green isle of Ireland and in Australia. In fact, I now have evidence that a deed exists, in grandfather's name, for land near a remote town called Stuart, near Alice Springs. I intend to make my way there and continue to untangle the mystery of the family curse that my brother so staunchly refuses to acknowledge. God knows, I pray he is right!

    I write you from the middle of the continent, continuing with Dr. Washburn's expedition. We have become quite friendly with the aboriginal people of the area, and these primitive folk guide us as to where we can find our next collection of cave paintings. It is quite a thrill to carry crude torches into these dark caverns and to view the ancient and often savage paintings that tell the story of these people. I use my artistic gift to sketch these depictions into my journal. We engage in many stimulating conversations about the possible meaning of this primitive art, while at the same time, I continue to piece together important information about the missing years our grandfather spent here on the continent down under.

So, dear sister-in-law, if you do not receive word from me in the coming months, do not fret— we are far from civilized culture and anyplace where a letter might be posted! I pray this finds its way to you, sent via the kindness of a rancher trekking through the region.

Love to my dear niece and to your handsome sailor!

—Pru

PS—As I always beg—despite Edward's pooh-poohing—please see that my brother takes care and caution in everything he does—particularly on the water. His safety is my greatest concern.

I grasped the letter so tightly that the edges curled in my sweaty hands.

Family curse? Their grandfather's—my great-grandfather's—missing years in Australia? And the postscript . . .

My eyes stung with tears of sadness and anger. Yes, Aunt Pru, how right you were to worry! In the time it took for her words to travel across the wide oceans and into my hands, her beloved brother and sister-in-law had perished.

I frantically shuffled through the rest of the stack, skimming, scanning.

Postcards from Boston and Newport from family, friends, and neighbors, filled with meaningless pleasantries. Thank-you notes from acquaintances, invitations to tea. A letter, five years old, from Aunt Pru, sent from Rome, describing the Colosseum and catacombs. Nothing else—just the terrible omen of a family curse come to pass!

Might it be that Pru was dead as well? I myself had only narrowly escaped an untimely end out there with Mother and Father. Perhaps I would be the next to suffer the Simmons family curse. I dropped my head to my knees and closed my eyes. A dark, thrilling thought crept into my brain. Maybe the curse would claim Uncle Victor. I shook the notion from my mind, ashamed of myself.

It was all too much to take in, following the mysterious incident in the library, the drama on the shore. I gathered the letters strewn about me and tied them back in a bundle, except for the only one that mattered. That one I slipped safely beneath the layers of my mattress. The remaining stack I shoved into the deep recesses of my wardrobe chest.

What to do . . . what to do?

My mind raced wildly. But my eyes were heavy.

Tomorrow, I thought, as I snuffed the wick of the lamp and fell into bed, tomorrow perhaps I would make some sense of it.

✶

The following days blurred together, one running over into the next, each day filled with anxious thoughts and musings. But one summer day was different—we had visitors. At the sound of the ship's bell tolling, Uncle Victor ran to the window and peered out. "Who in the devil . . . ," he began. "Addie! Addie, go and find out what they want!"

I followed her to the door. My school chum Emma Pratt stood there dressed in her Sunday best, staring down at her fine button shoes, a bunch of daisies clenched in her fist. Mrs. Pratt wore a pitying expression and held out a blueberry pie in her white-gloved hands. She nodded toward me but looked at Addie. "It was high time we came to offer our condolences," she said. "Isn't it, Emma?" She nudged Emma with her elbow. "Emma!"

Emma didn't look up. "I'm very sorry about your . . . um . . . loss," she mumbled. Mrs. Pratt nodded and smiled in a pinched way. "Given the fact that there wasn't really a funeral, or calling hours, we waited until things were, well, settled. . . ."

I didn't know what to say, but Addie saved me. "Well, isn't that sweet of ye; now come in, come in." She gestured in an expansive way, took the pie from Mrs. Pratt, and led them inside.

"Mr. Simmons, sir," she called, "Mrs. Pratt and her lovely Emma have come to pay their respects. I'll put on the tea." She turned. "Lucy, show our guests to the parlor now, would ye?"

We sat awkwardly on the settee. Emma looked at me, finally. "So, what's it like to be a *real* live orphan?" she blurted.

"Emma!" Mrs. Pratt exclaimed. "What a thing to say!"

I felt my face color. At that moment Aunt Margaret sashayed in, followed by Uncle Victor.

"Afternoon," Aunt Margaret crooned. I noticed she'd changed her dress and was wearing a lot of jewelry. Mother's jewelry! My mouth dropped open. Uncle Victor crossed his arms and rocked back on his heels.

"I'm Victor Simmons, and this is my wife, Margaret. We are in charge of this place now that my dear brother and his lovely wife have tragically passed on. Still in mourning, aren't we, Margaret?"

Victor's smile and the sparkle in his eyes told a different story. Aunt Margaret, dabbing at her eyes, was, to me at least, equally unconvincing.

Just as Addie started through the door with the silver tea service, Victor stepped in front of her, stopping her short.

"Given that the household is still grieving," he said, "I do suggest we postpone this little visit. You understand, of course."

Mrs. Pratt's long white face turned pink as she stood and took Emma by the hand.

"I promise we shall not be disturbing you again," she said. "Come along, Emma!"

Emma looked over her shoulder at me, trying, I imagined, to get one last look at a real orphan.

"Toodle-oo!" Aunt Margaret cried as the door closed behind them. "Appreciate the pie!"

I could imagine them walking down the front path, the look of distaste pulling at the corners of their mouths.

"We'll have no more uninvited guests snooping around here," Victor said. "Next time, Addie, you will turn them away! Now, out of my sight!"

Addie turned on her heel and disappeared into the kitchen, the door swinging behind her.

Still, I was relieved. I couldn't bear to have any more of my friends meet my aunt and uncle, to see what shameful, ungracious people they were.

As if sensing my relief, Uncle Victor shifted his beady eyes in my direction. "What are you standing there gaping at? There are chores to be done, missy! You'll thank me someday for teaching you the value of hard work! Now get on with the dusting!"

I turned toward the broom closet, grateful for anything to get me away from him.

"And don't forgot the bathroom!" he shouted.

I took the feather duster from its hook and headed for the dining room, lost in my own musings. It was as though, in lieu of family and school chums, the house had become my companion, my ally. I leaned my forehead against the cool oak paneling in the hall and closed my eyes. "I need you," I whispered, my breath leaving a moist circle on the polished surface. I paused, listening for the quiet breathing of the house, feeling for that sense of life that had pulsed through it on that peculiar night. Stranger still, I believed the house actually *responded* to my recognition of its energy, its soul. My cheek tingled, and even behind my closed lids I was dazzled by starbursts of color. I was suddenly infused with a giddy burst of energy, a high-spirited sense of fun.

I bounded off, the feather duster a magical wand in my hand. I waved it with a flourish along the wainscoting in the dining room and up along the edge of the tall built-in corner cupboard. I sang as I worked, *"A la dee dah dah, a la dee dah dee!"* But the top ledge of the cabinetry was beyond my reach. As I stretched on tiptoes in an attempt to complete the chore, the ledge began to glow—not a wild, garish shine, mind you, rather a low-luster, good-natured sort of twinkle, and the cabinet bent over, ever so slightly in a courtly bow, just enough to meet the ruffled tips of my feathery wand. I waved the duster in a salute, giggled, and moved on.

With unbounded energy I fairly skipped to the basement to retrieve the bucket and scrub brush, star water, and sponge, and lugged them back upstairs. Suddenly, the prospect of scrubbing the tile floor and shining the brass fixtures of the lavatory seemed like an adventure. I ran the water, assembled my supplies, and began with the sink. In seconds it was gleaming. Then I approached the deep claw-footed tub. But I'd left the metal bucket and the scrub brush on the opposite side of the room. I turned and stepped back for them, anticipating the strain of hauling the heavy pail of sloshing suds a step or two nearer. I hoisted the bucket in one hand, turned, then stopped short. The tub itself moved, its claw feet flexing slightly, inching along the black-and-white checkerboard floor until it snuggled up beside me.

I set the bucket down and grinned. As if to remind me of the task at hand, the smooth rolled edge of the tub curled over in a gentle curtsy-like dip—an invitation for me to do what I'd set out to do. I scrubbed, staring in amazement as the suds sparkled and swirled, encircling the inner perimeter, erasing the last trace of Uncle Victor's dull beige tub ring. The sparkling mist swirled into a neat funnel shape, and the small glittering tornado spun down the drain, leaving the tub gleaming. Then, just as I knew it would, the tub tiptoed back to its place. I applauded, and once more it curtsied.

Still marveling, I carried the bucket and scrub brush back to the cellar and set them down next to Father's "chart room." Here he'd built a platform on which he'd set his prized trophy from his last sea vessel—an enormous nautical wheel. I climbed up, grasped the knobs at the end of each rung just as Father'd once done. I closed my eyes and turned the wheel, imagining . . .

"Set our sights for Australia!" I shouted, feeling

anything was possible, spinning the wheel to the right. We'd sail the Eastern seaboard, past the islands, around Cape Horn, and across the South Pacific—eventually we'd hit Australia, wouldn't we?

I sang out, *"A la dee dah dah, a lah dee dah dee. . . ."* I could swear, as I sang, that the lilting tone of Father's flute accompanied my song. "Raise the sails full-tilt!" I commanded.

> *"With cutlass and gun, oh, we fought for hours three.*
> *Blow high! Blow low! And so sailed we.*
> *The ship it was their coffin, and their grave it was the sea!*
> *A-sailing down all on the coasts of High Barbaree.*
> *A la dee dah dah, a lah dee dah dee. . . ."*

The squeal of the winch and the flap of imaginary canvas against the wind bolstered my bravado. "We have a job to do! Find Miss Prudence Simmons and banish the *evil* Victor from his illustrious brother's estate!" One hand on the wheel, I raised the other in a defiant fist and shook it in the air.

Then, in a flash, a viselike grip on my wrist yanked me, not only from my imaginary drama at sea, but clear off the platform.

7

His face was beet red, his temples throbbing. He spoke to me through clenched teeth, lips curled back in a snarl.

"This is how you avoid your chores, is it, missy? Mocking the duty your aunt and I perform here, disrespecting us with your . . . your . . . theatrics?"

I thought my wrist might snap, he'd twisted it so far behind my back. I swallowed the cry that threatened to erupt from my throat. I wouldn't give him the satisfaction.

In his left hand he held a wire rug beater and raised it above his head. He shook it, in the same way I'd shaken my fist just moments before.

"There'll be a beating here today," he said, fairly spitting the words at me.

I braced myself for the blow when I heard Addie descend the stairs. He released my wrist, glared, and thrust the rug beater at me.

"Take this and the hallway runner outside and beat it until it's clean. Do you understand me, missy?"

Addie stopped at the bottom of the stairs, her eyes wide at his icy tone of voice. "And one more thing," he said. He turned toward Addie. "You'll see to it that this wench stays out of the cellar." He turned to me. "Now, *get out*!"

I flew up the stairs, rug beater in hand, and grabbed the hallway runner from the floor. Aunt Margaret, who had a way of slinking around eavesdropping, clearly had overheard the whole exchange. She smugly shoved a basket of darning into my other hand.

"While you're at it," she said, and turned on her heel.

I set out toward the water, Mr. Pugsley trotting along behind me. My hands were still trembling, and the white anger I'd felt toward Victor was finally dissipating, turning my joints to jelly.

Yet, as always, the sight of the sea and the feel of

the ocean air bolstered my spirit. I loved the ruffle of white foam curling around the shore on the crest of the waves, the way the water slipped in between the rocky crevices and was sucked back, over and over again. Down, down we hiked, along the rocky path toward the shore, each step stronger and more determined than the previous. The hypnotic tune found its way to my lips still again—*"A la dee dah dah, a la dee dah dee"*—perhaps because it was the last tune Father and I sang together. How I wished I knew the rest of the lyrics.

My eyes were suddenly drawn to a small strip of shore where the water glittered brilliantly and bubbled over a narrow ribbon of sand, skirting a number of black rocks. I paused beside a slight dip in the ground sheltered by rosebushes, a spot unseen from the path. I shoved the carpet, the beater, and the basket of needlework inside the fragrant hideaway and continued on, drawn to the place that seemed to be churning diamonds in the surf. I stepped quickly, deftly, off the path, rock to ledge, stone to stone, down, down, down toward the hypnotizing tide, so dazzling now that I had to shield my eyes with my hand. The surf rushed in, splashing over my shoes and the edges of my skirts, but still I pressed on, inexplicably drawn to the spot. Between the surge and slosh of the sea, I heard something else that my heart recognized before I could name it. I froze. It was the sound of Father's flute, playing that tune that refused to leave my mind! I looked down. Gasped.

Upon hitting the rocks beneath me, the incoming waves burst into a million sparkling particles that curled and tingled around my feet and ankles. The gleaming vaporous mass crested for an instant and ebbed, receding with the tide.

But there at my feet, balanced precariously on the craggy rock, was Father's flute, delivered up from the sea! It dripped salt water and diamond glitter, still playing the tune of its own accord. It hummed, tingled. *A la dee dah dah, a la dee dah dee*—each note carried by a lilt and puff of sparkling vapor like the breath of a phantom flautist. I bent, snatched it up, put it to my lips, my fingers drawn to the tone holes. Guided by an unknown force, I began to play. At the end of the refrain I stopped, incredulous, and held the flute out before me.

Mr. Pugsley whined, and his small curlicue tail began wagging frantically. His paws slipped and slid on the slick stones. "What is it, Mr. Pugsley?" I asked, with some alarm. Someone must be near! With trembling hands I placed the precious flute deep in my pocket for safekeeping. Mr. Pugsley's little rump wiggled side to side, and he shot ahead.

I grabbed him just in time, held his wriggling body against me, and leaned forward for a look.

There she was, just down the shore, different in the afternoon light, but somehow still the same. She walked smoothly toward the water in a regal way. This was no idle stroll—her movements were strong and purposeful.

Her silver hair was pulled back in a neat braid, her limbs long and graceful. I was certain that the gray robe she wore was the very same one she'd wrapped around herself on the night of the full moon. As she reached the water's edge, she looked around as if to make certain she was not being watched, and let the robe slip from her shoulders.

I covered my mouth with my hand. She wore nothing at all beneath the robe, and in her nakedness moved surely, confidently into the sea. The only sign that the water was cold was a slight hunching of her shoulders, and a slow lifting and lengthening of her neck above the water.

She glided out with strong, sure strokes, her braid trailing the surface like a sleek water snake. She swam for a bit, then floated, occasionally diving underwater, resurfacing with a blink of her eyes, her mouth open for a wide gulp of air.

I held Mr. Pugsley tight and carried him up, up, back to the rosebush hideaway, where I could watch without being detected. I lifted the branches and quickly ducked inside. The hanging boughs sur-rounded me in tangled masses, dotted with small, dense deep-pink roses. I pushed one aside, creat-ing a peephole, and there—I spotted the old woman still swimming with confident, smooth strokes.

Something farther down the thin strip of sandy beach caught my eye. Not wanting to take my eyes off the woman, I stole a glance in the other direction.

Mr. Pugsley saw it too, the short tawny hair on his back bristling in alarm. Holding his squirming body close, I felt the low rumble of his growl and the rapid drumroll of his heart.

It was the Brute, barreling across the beach. He called out to the woman in a menacing voice, words carried off by the ocean breeze, hands waving above his head.

She became immediately alert, interrupted her stroke, and drew herself up like a curious otter. Did I just imagine her eyes narrowing, or did I actually see it? She dived forward and swam in a straight line toward the shore. This I watched with a sense of impending danger, as it was clear the Brute was closer to her robe than she was.

That was when Mr. Pugsley shoved off against me with his small sturdy legs and projected himself out of the rosebush and onto the trail.

"No, Mr. Pugsley!" I shouted, but as I moved to follow him, I stopped short. No one knew of my hiding place, and I could not reveal it to the Brute. Biting my lip, I pulled back and watched as Mr. Pugsley tore down the path, kicking up clouds of dust in his wake.

The Brute slowed to a stop and turned—first his head, then his entire frame—in the direction of the little beast. "No, Mr. Pugsley," I whispered. "Stay away from him!" Tears welled up in my eyes. I was ashamed that my terror held me back, that I was powerless to intervene for my canine friend.

"Is that you, you ungrateful . . . ," the Brute began, the rest of his ugly words lost to the wind. He lunged at Mr. Pugsley, but the little dog was too nimble for him, passing around behind him, nipping at the legs of his ragged pants.

"You son of the devil . . ."

The Brute bent over and swept his hand in a powerful arc toward the dog and kicked wildly in an attempt to shake Mr. Pugsley free of his pants.

The sight of the woman slipping into the gray robe was almost lost to me, so engaged was I in poor Mr. Pugsley's fate. I watched, scarcely breathing, as the Brute stomped his feet around my little friend, and I nearly cheered as Mr. Pugsley let go at precisely the right moment, scooting back between the giant's legs. Trying to keep the little fellow in his sights, the Brute spun about, and must have lost his balance on the thin strand of slippery rocks, driftwood, and debris that edged the shore. He went down like a felled tree, and Mr. Pugsley took the opportunity to grab his shirtsleeve, shaking it violently back and forth. He must have connected with skin, because amid the growling and the tearing of cloth, I heard the Brute cry out and grab at his arm.

The little dog trotted back, head raised high, clearly proud of his work. Before the man could right himself, Mr. Pugsley scrambled off, disappearing into the tall grass that ran along the shore.

I sank back in relief, but only for an instant. I watched the Brute peering about, and that was when we made the discovery together—that both the old woman and the dog were gone. I followed the Brute's crazed gaze to the water's edge, to the place where her robe had been.

He turned this way and that, eyes furtively searching the shore as well as the cliffs above. "I'll get you yet," he shouted, "you sea hag, you, you . . . witch of the water!" He raised his fist high, gesturing wildly, calling out into the salty air. I stayed perfectly still, watching as his eyes skimmed past my hiding place, and followed his retreat into the knoll of pines until he disappeared altogether. I stared out for what seemed like hours, desperately looking for Mr. Pugsley, and wondering where on earth the old woman had gone.

Suddenly I felt a firm hand on my shoulder. Without thinking I jumped to my feet, the thorny branches scratching my face, yanking my hair. I gasped. My hiding place was no longer a secret.

8

"Shhh!" she said, crouching down and pushing past me into the hideout. I stared, openmouthed. "Who . . . ? What?" I stammered.

"Shhh!" she repeated, more vehemently.

I gaped at her holding Mr. Pugsley tightly against her chest. Her eyes were fixed straight ahead, staring through the space in the bushes.

"Sit down, sit down!" she whispered, flapping her hand like the wing of a bird. I knelt alongside her, shamelessly studying her strong profile. Wispy silver strands had escaped her braid and hung along the sides of her face, reminding me of the side feathers on an Indian headdress. Her skin was a warm honey brown, sun-weathered and deeply lined. A long, straight nose was chiseled in between high cheekbones—all of which completed the look of an Indian brave. Her eyes were quite riveting— the palest shade of green—and staring at them from the side made me think of a pair of shiny aqua marbles. In the hollow of her throat hung a large oval silver locket.

I watched her expression change from rapt attention to one of slight amusement, the skin around those fine eyes crinkling, the corners of her mouth turning slightly up. She cast a quick glance my way, nodded outward with her chin in the direction of the path, and then raised a long, bony index finger to her lips as a reminder for silence. She tipped her head, a motion that made me listen more closely.

That was when I detected a weak huffing sound out along the path. She raised an eyebrow at me and I nodded, acknowledging that we both heard it. The huffing got louder, raspier, an escalating series of ragged pants and gasps. I knew even before I saw him—it was the Brute climbing the steep trail in pursuit of the woman he'd called a sea hag, a witch of the sea. The woman I was crouching beside, who had my dog in her arms.

And, I might add, I felt more than a tinge of

jealousy at Mr. Pugsley's carrying on. There he was in her arms, flirting in the way he usually reserved for me, blinking his long-lashed brown eyes adoringly, nudging her hand with his nose, looking for a pat on the head, snuggling as close as he could. And, not only that—as the Brute emerged over the summit, I'd have expected a barrage of yipping and ferocious growling, but Mr. Pugsley behaved like a docile lamb.

This was a good thing, because the Brute placed himself like a sentinel at the top of the trail, not fifteen feet from where we hid, shielding his eyes from the sun and peering down toward the shore. He muttered under his breath, and shook his head of wild black hair in agitation. I strained to hear the snippets of his utterings that drifted toward us: "playing with magic," "swimming like a siren," "the singing of a sea nymph."

We both knew whom he was referring to. She gave me a quick glance, her eyes amused, one corner of her mouth pulled up in a half smile, an eyebrow raised. The smile I returned felt stiff and peculiar on my face.

The Brute's words disturbed me. Not the babbling about playing with magic. No. It was the part about the sirens—the sea nymphs—that sent a chill along my spine. I remembered all too well

Father's tales of these mythical sea creatures whose haunting songs charmed seamen to leap into the sea to their deaths. I recalled the painting back in our library of Ulysses, the famous Greek mariner bound to the mast of his ship in order to resist the sirens' death call.

I couldn't help but wonder whether my own father, and perhaps the Brute himself, had heard such a call on that fateful day. Or whether the Brute's words had something to do with the terrible curse Aunt Pru referred to. Those thoughts continued to pull at the edges of my brain, the image of that painting I'd always found fascinating—in a dark, foreboding way—nudging me. It was as if there was something important I was missing, something almost understood but just beyond my grasp. At that moment I felt the flute tingle against my skin through the lining in my pocket. Or perhaps it was a shiver.

The Brute, apparently satisfied that the woman had vanished, threw up his hands and started off again down the path. We watched him trudge along the zigzagging trail until he reached the shore. He stared across the water for some time before moving down the beach and into the pine grove in the distance.

The woman put Mr. Pugsley down and turned to me.

"So," she said, her voice rather low-pitched, smooth, and warm, "we finally meet, face-to-face—officially, that is."

To this, I said nothing, although I imagine I probably nodded stupidly.

"Well, come along then," she said.

Without waiting for my reply, she crawled out through the opening in the rosebush.

Mr. Pugsley darted out beside her, his eagerness grating on me more than a little. I followed along behind. I felt a pang of guilt over the fact that I was excited. It seemed disloyal to Mother and Father to be enjoying things in their absence. This was something, after all—something happening to me that buoyed me up out of the sea of sadness pulling me under.

"So," she said, her voice deep and rich, "how are you surviving?" She reached over and gently brushed the hair from my face. Curiously, she ran her finger over the scar on my forehead and nodded, as if pleased.

"Uh . . . ," I stammered, "well, I . . ."

"Since the accident," she added. "How are you getting along is what I want to know?"

I felt my face flush. "How do you know about the accident? How do you know who I am?"

She looked at me kindly. "Well, dear, everyone

along the coast knows of the tragic event. I'm quite certain I remember the day more clearly than most."

"Well," I said, flustered, "I suppose I'm doing . . . all right."

It was all I could manage. Nibbling the inside of my cheek, I stared at her, questions gnawing at me. I believe she understood quite a bit more than I actually offered.

"You are a brave and unusual sort, Lucy P. Simmons," she said.

I felt as though I had passed some kind of test. This bolstered my courage, and my words came in a rush.

"But, who are *you*? I don't remember ever seeing you about town, or out here by the shore until, well . . . since . . ." I avoided the words with a shake of my head. "I've watched you at night, out in the moonlight. That's when things started to—" I stopped abruptly. Perhaps I'd said too much.

She looked straight ahead, then put her finger to her lips, silencing me. Mr. Pugsley stood still and began to whimper. I followed her gaze and, to my great dismay, saw Uncle Victor clambering along the path.

"It's my unc—" I stopped short. The woman had moved off the path and was weaving in and out of the pines. Mr. Pugsley watched her intently, and for a moment I feared he might run off after her. But my faithful friend stood there beside me. I stared after her, fighting the urge to call out. She nodded at me, with a slow blink of her green eyes. It was a gesture of assurance that set my mind at ease, at least for the moment. As she disappeared into the trees, I looked back toward Uncle Victor, his thin legs carrying him swiftly toward me.

"What are you doing dawdling out here on the path?" he demanded. "And where, pray tell, is the carpet? Your aunt nearly slipped in the hallway!"

Before I could answer, he went on. "And who was that I heard you talking with?" He peered this way and that through narrowed eyes. "Answer me, missy!" he said.

"Which question?" I asked, and rather rudely, I might add. Something about my encounter with the woman had emboldened me.

"Which *question*?" he bellowed. He sputtered for a moment, apparently unsure himself. "What do you think you're doing dawdling out here, when you have chores to do? I asked you what you were doing, is what I asked!"

I looked at him in what I hoped was an innocent manner. "I was . . ." I hesitated. But what with the appearance of Father's flute, the Brute, and then the woman, well, I was at a loss. "I was . . . airing out the carpet," I said quickly. "And doing my needlework."

As soon as I said it, I knew I'd made a mistake. I'd left both the runner and my basket of sewing inside my hideaway, forgotten.

Uncle Victor looked at me closely, his nostrils twitching like a hound picking up a scent. "Really? And where exactly is the carpet now?"

I bit my lower lip. "It . . . it was airing out on the rocky outcropping there, and I dozed off in the sun and . . . and . . . I think a bluster of wind may have carried it off?"

He circled around me, looking me up and down. "That, my dear niece, is a blatant lie! Absolute poppycock! Hogwash! Just look at you!"

My hand went instinctively to smooth my hair, my skirts. I was suddenly painfully aware of the soaked and filthy hemline of my dress, of my black button shoes now encrusted in mud. I ran my hand across my forehead in an attempt to tidy myself and was appalled to see a streak of red on my fingers. I'd forgotten how I'd entangled myself in the rosebush, how I'd gotten scratched. I felt the color rise to my cheeks at the memory of my hair being yanked by the branches, and could only imagine how wild it must be, hanging from my ribbons as it was.

None of this escaped Uncle Victor, who grabbed me roughly by the arm. "You might have gotten away with behaving like a wild Indian living under my brother's roof," he hissed, "but you'll not act as a banshee living here with me!" He shoved me along the path, his skinny fingers pressing into my arm like a vise. Mr. Pugsley ran around, circling wildly, yipping in protest.

"I'll have to have a word with your aunt about this," Uncle Victor said, shaking his head and wagging a long finger in the air. I tripped along beside him, cringing at the scene I knew would follow—a perfect opportunity for Uncle Victor to bully both me and Aunt Margaret at the same time. It would be doubly bad for me, of course, for once he was done with Margaret, she would take her frustration out on me as well.

As we approached the house, I was captivated by the sunlight playing off of the front stairs that led to the wide wraparound porch. The afternoon light seemed dappled, dancing across the steps, like sunlight on water. But as we got closer, I grew more excited. It was not ordinary sunlight playing on the stairs. It was sparkling, glittering. I chanced a glance at Uncle Victor, who marched on, unaware, his eye trained on the front door.

I held my breath as he dragged me toward

the first step, my eyes cast downward. I felt the electricity at my feet and blinked at the wavy lines of energy—like heat shimmering on a paved road baking in the sun—that I saw emanating from that wavering step. I watched as Uncle Victor's side of the wooden step grew, as though drawn up in the flow of energy surrounding it. Just as he lifted his foot to scale the step, the flute vibrated, and something like the shrill cry of a bird flew from it and pierced the air. Victor swiveled his head, eyebrows raised. The vapor seeped along the base of the stair, and just as he stepped up, the floorboards bulged.

The jolt of his shoe meeting the swollen step sent him flying forward. He released my arm and I sprang up the stairs and out of his grasp, Mr. Pugsley beside me.

I heard the clunk of his nose against the upper stair, and the shower of curses that followed. The flute huffed and puffed a ruffle of tuneless air ticklishly against me. I immediately recognized it as the cadence of laughter, and stifled the *gahuff* that threatened to spring from my lips.

Aunt Margaret barreled past me, her eyes opened wide, fleshy cheeks jiggling, hands grasping the edges of her apron.

"What on earth?" she chirped, her words coming in nervous bursts.

I shrugged a little and watched Mr. Pugsley run to his hiding space beneath the stairwell. "I guess he tripped," I said, and rushed toward the library.

I closed the door behind me, shutting out Uncle Victor's demands for an ice pack, some brandy (he was always boasting of the medicinal qualities of brandy, after all), a bandage, a cigar.

I walked slowly toward the painting that hung on the wall opposite the window and stood before it. The blood pulsed in my temples, and my heart hammered against my chest.

There was Ulysses tied to the mast of his ship, his wild eyes raised toward the sky. He was the focal point of the painting, the part that drew your eye and held it.

But this time I forced myself to look, *really* look at the rest of the painting—at the huge white moon that illuminated Ulysses's fear, casting a ghostly path across the water—and in that path, the head of the siren, the sea nymph, radiating like a star in a black sea-sky.

I picked up the ivory-handled magnifying glass from Father's desk and approached the painting. With trembling hands I held the glass up, and the circle behind it sprang into view, increasing impressively in both size and detail.

The wavy-edged image in the glass fairly

sparkled as it tripled in size. And I stared at the siren in the moonlit sea approaching the ship, her silvery hair streaming out behind her.

I shook my head and stepped away from the painting. Perhaps my imagination was getting the better of me, but the siren in the painting and the woman on the path could have been one and the same.

9

In my room I waited out the storm. Standing
before my dressing table, I retrieved my
precious flute, rolled it over and over in my hands,
and brought it to my lips. I kissed it, and placed
it on the bureau cloth. A large looking glass hung
behind the dressing table, and catching sight of my
appearance, I gasped.

I'd always been told how much I resembled
Mother, with her serene blue eyes and auburn
hair. But at that moment, it was not the ghost of
my mother that stared back at me—it was more like
my Aunt Prudence, more mischievous than Mother

for sure, and yes, maybe even a little reckless. My sweaty face was smeared with dirt. My hair, which Addie usually arranged in waves held off of my face with fine ribbons, was mussed and tangled, a halo of reddish curls and frizz. Small leaves were stuck here and there, even a thin twig or two. These I gingerly pulled out and hid in my pocket.

There was a knock on the door, followed by my aunt's waffling voice, even higher pitched than usual.

"I need a word with you, Lucille. Open the door and let me inside!"

I attempted to wipe off my face and pull my hair into some kind of shape before opening the door. I sat on the edge of my bed and looked down, trying to appear repentant.

Aunt Margaret stood directly before me, twisting the sash of her dress nervously around her plump fingers. She was positioned so that glancing up put me at eye level with her massive bosom. I looked back down and waited.

"What in heaven's name were you up to out there?" she asked. Her voice was whining, wheedling. "Now you've gone and got your uncle all upset," and as if to justify the irritation in her voice, she quickly added, "And I can't say that I blame him! What do you have to say for yourself?"

I mumbled an apology. "I'm sorry, Aunt Margaret," I said. "I didn't mean to cause any trouble."

"Well, you'll have to go down and tell him that yourself," said Aunt Margaret, who by now was pacing back and forth, her lower lip curled over like a spoiled child's. "Now you've got him in a tizzy."

And, as if his tizzy needed explanation, she added, "He's in a lot of pain, thanks to that little dog of yours."

"What do you mean, thanks to my little dog?"

Aunt Margaret paused. "For tripping him on the step," she said, annoyance bending the pitch of her last word up a tone or two.

I suddenly paid more attention. If he blamed Mr. Pugsley for this fall, would he decide to get rid of him?

"Aunt Margaret," I said, "it wasn't Mr. Pugsley's fault. It was my fault."

"Yes, it was," she said, her bottom lip still curled out, her rolls of chin held high. "He is your dog, after all, and your uncle is nice enough to let you keep him!"

"No," I said. "No, Mr. Pugsley didn't trip Uncle Victor. It was *my* fault, it was my . . . my . . ." I struggled for something that would work, my eyes scanning the room for some clue.

"What was it then?" asked Aunt Margaret. I detected movement just behind her, and to my surprise the flute was levitating above the dresser! Incredulous, my eyes followed it floating around the bookshelf, dancing above the commode and washstand, and finally making its descent toward the bowl of marbles atop my desk. There it hovered and dipped, pointing and jabbing repeatedly at the collection of cat's-eyes and jaspers, aggies and opals. That was it! Of course!

Without thinking, I wagged my finger accusingly at the bowl of marbles. The flute rapidly dipped behind the bowl, out of sight.

"I told Uncle Victor I was out doing needlework and airing the carpet," I blustered. "But I wasn't. I was out playing marbles, out on a flat place on the path," I said, gathering energy as the excuse grew. "And then, coming back, I dropped one—yes, that's it—I dropped a marble on the step, and Uncle Victor must have slipped on it!"

I was so excited that I'd been led to fabricate a tale to save my little friend that I almost smiled. Addie suddenly appeared in the doorway, watching me curiously.

Aunt Margaret frowned. "He was right then," she said, pouting. "You *did* lie to him!" She made a series of tsk-tsk sounds with her tongue. "Well, that will make it all the worse for you, I'm sure. He's resting in the library. You'd best go and see him, missy, and be ready to take your punishment."

"I'll go along, ma'am, and see that she behaves," said Addie, making a show of ushering me out the door. Aunt Margaret nodded, pleased, I'm sure, to be addressed as the lady of the house. I looked at Addie appreciatively, for I understood her intent. I would be punished less severely in her presence.

She held my elbow gently as we walked down the stairs, tipped her head slightly toward mine, and whispered in my ear. "Maybe, lass, you'll be tellin' me what 'twas you were actually doin'," she said, not unkindly, concern warming her words.

The library door was open and Uncle Victor saw us coming. He made quite a show of pulling himself upright. My eyes widened at the sight of his bruised and battered face. His nose had a large bump about halfway down, looking as though one of those marbles I'd lied about had been jammed up there beneath his skin. The area around his eye was swollen an angry red with the promise that by tomorrow it would turn black and blue.

"You are dismissed, miss," he said to Addie, the iciness in his voice sending a shiver along my spine.

"I thought I would stay, sir," she said evenly, "in order that I might help in maintaining the discipline of my young charge here."

"I *said*, you are dismissed!"

Addie gave my arm a little squeeze, and I watched her mouth pull into a straight line. "But, sir—"

"Out!" he yelled, the snaky veins in the side of his head throbbing.

Addie nodded and slid silently out the door.

"Close it!" he bellowed. I watched Addie take a deep breath and gently shut the door.

Uncle Victor walked toward me. Though not a big man, he was taller than me, and he leaned over so that his bruised face was just inches from my own.

"This," he said, pointing to his face, "this is your doing! You and that miserable dog of yours."

"No!" I began. "No, you don't underst—"

"Silence!"

I not only heard the word, but felt the force of his breath explode against my face. I backed up, my mouth dry, hands shaking.

"I have a good mind to have the beast drowned, as he should have been in the first place!"

I thought, at that point, that my legs might give way, that I might actually pass out. Would the water swallow up everyone and everything I loved? Mother, Father, Mr. Pugsley? I pushed back the sorrow that rose up in me like a squall.

"No," I pleaded, "it wasn't Mr. Pugsley's fault."

"Shut up," he snarled. "You, missy, are not going to make a fool of me! And we won't be spoiling you rotten like those putting-on-airs parents of yours were so fond of doing! Oh no! There'll be no more of that, I can assure you. A little liar, you are, an ill-bred little ruffian."

"You're right, Uncle Victor," I said, almost choking on the words, furious that he'd insulted my wonderful parents, but I pressed on.

"I did lie. I wasn't out there doing my chores. You were right. I was playing marbles, is what I was doing."

I thrust a handful of the clear aqua and agate marbles under his nose. "See! I was using these. I dropped one on the path and when I went to pick it up I stumbled. That's how I got dirty and scratched."

The words poured out, one lie after the next. "And then . . . and then . . . . out here on the steps I dropped one, and, and . . . you stepped on it, I'm sure of it. That's how you tripped. I am so, so sorry," I lied, allowing the tears of fear and anger I felt at the prospect of losing Mr. Pugsley to slip down my cheeks.

"I never wanted to see you get hurt," I sobbed,

channeling my frustration into my role as penitent. "I'm *very* sorry. Please, please don't punish the dog. It wasn't his fault!"

I covered my face with my hands and chanced a glance through the tangle of hair and dirty fingers. Uncle Victor stared at me with an odd mix of anger and satisfaction—satisfaction, I'm sure, in thinking that he'd broken my spirit.

He pulled the thin smile that spread across his lips into a grimace and lifted my chin so that I was once again eye to eye, nose to nose with him.

"Listen to me, missy," he said. "There'll be no more lying. There'll be no more dillydallying out there near the shore. No more of your shenanigans."

"But Mr. Pugsley . . ."

"I'll let you keep the dog—for *now*," he emphasized. "But the *next* time you disobey me, or dishonor me with a lie, the beast goes; do you understand that?"

"Yes," I said, nodding, "yes, I understand." Relief almost bowled me over.

He took a step back from me and pointed his finger in my face.

"You, young lady—although you don't deserve that title—will *not* be allowed outdoors."

I gasped.

"But . . . ," I struggled, "but what about . . ."

My distress seemed to make him more adamant. "You are not to venture outside without my ex*press* permission, do you understand that?"

I nodded, knowing I had no choice.

"Then we understand each other," he said. "I spare the dog, for the moment, and you answer to me. I would say that, under the circumstances, that is quite generous on my part. Now, go upstairs, missy, and do not come down until tomorrow. You will do without your dinner. Do you understand?"

I nodded again.

"Now go," he said, with a flick of his hand. "Out of my sight!"

I turned and left the room, walking silently past Addie and Aunt Margaret, stationed outside the door.

As I crossed the threshold into my room, I knew I had indeed crossed another line—and had come to a curiously exhilarating, yet frightening, realization.

In order to find Aunt Pru, rescue our home, and protect my loyal Mr. Pugsley, I would consciously and determinedly disobey—and yes—even lie to Uncle Victor when circumstances required it, as I suspected they most certainly would.

I offered a silent apology to Mother and Father—after all, they hadn't raised me to be dishonest or disobedient. This I followed with a vow to do whatever I had to do, hoping, believing, that Mother and Father would understand.

10

The very next day I stood before my bedroom window, staring toward the shore. I'd already spent some time playing Father's flute. The notes of the chantey were now confidently beneath my fingers, the tone pure and clear. There were times, however, when the instrument seemed to play of its own accord, ornamenting and embellishing the simple tunes I was capable of—or perhaps it was my imagination working overtime, bored as I was as a prisoner in my own house. I laid my precious flute down on the windowsill and gazed longingly outside.

There had to be a way to earn Uncle Victor's confidence, or at least a way to convince him to allow me out of doors. I ran down a list of tedious outdoor chores that might sound virtuous to him— weeding the garden, picking rose hips out along the shore. I even thought of suggesting clamming, for I knew he loved to slurp raw clams from the half shell. The problem with that notion was that I hadn't the faintest idea of how to collect clams—I knew it involved digging in the mud, but beyond that, I hadn't a clue.

While muddling through these schemes, I caught a glimpse of a most amazing sight down on the bumpy old shore road—a wide dirt path, really, that was the only link between our small peninsula and the village. A squarish wagon, drawn by a swaybacked old brown horse, made its way lazily along, raising a cloud of dust beneath its large spoked wheels. The wagon itself was painted black, the letters RFD emblazoned on the side in fancy red-and-gold script.

My heart thumped wildly. I had heard Father speak of his efforts to bring the mail wagon—the Rural Free Delivery—to our home and to the other remote homes along the shore, for up until that time, receiving mail required a trip into the village to the postal office. The carefully constructed wooden mailbox Father made had stood at the edge of our property along the shore road for perhaps a year awaiting the promised Rural Free Delivery. But the mail wagon had never come—at least not until now. At this very moment, I surmised, the postman might be carrying a letter from Aunt Prudence—a letter he would place in our mailbox! There was a small red-hinged flag on the side of the box that remained inconspicuously tucked in place. But when the postman placed mail in the box, he would lift the flag—a signal that mail had arrived. And I further surmised that Uncle Victor would notice that flag in an instant and be upon the box, the letter, and the key to my freedom in the blink of an eye. I had to get to the box before he noticed—I *had* to!

My first thought was to tiptoe down the staircase and out the front door. But there was no way to know whether Uncle Victor was sitting in the front parlor, in view of the door; in the library, which was set off to the side; or even on the front porch. I would just have to take a chance.

As I stepped toward my bedroom door, a curious dizzy feeling came over me. The door seemed to spin before my eyes, and to my great dismay, despite all of my pulling and yanking, the door would not budge! The glass knob slipped in my sweaty palms, and the door seemed to actually swell up stubbornly in its frame. I furiously twisted, jiggled, and tugged at the crystal knob, but the door remained resolutely shut.

A faint tinkling noise over near the window interrupted my efforts. I turned to face the sound and found another of those swirling, glittering clouds floating about my bedroom window. I stood staring as the mist seeped between the window and the ledge, and watched the window slide effortlessly open. Father's flute slowly floated on the mist and began to play, coaxing me, calling me, as though played by an invisible Pied Piper.

Mesmerized, I stepped forward. The flute dipped and bobbed in encouragement, the tune increasing in tempo. The instrument tipped and pointed toward the window. I followed, staring out through the wavy glass pane.

The mail wagon was rounding the bend toward Father's mailbox. To my chagrin, the postman began ringing a bell to herald the arrival of the much-awaited RFD service. As if in response, Father's ship's bell clanged as well. It would only be a matter of time before Uncle Victor went to investigate the cacophony.

There was a knock on my door, followed by Addie's voice.

"Here you go, darlin'," she called. "I've got yer breakfast tray ready for ye."

I rushed to the door and pressed my lips against the keyhole.

"Addie," I whispered, the desperation somehow carrying my hushed voice out to her. "Addie, be very quiet! Don't say anything that will arouse their attention!"

I was met with silence.

"Addie!" I said, as loud as I dared. "Addie?"

"Yes, Lucy," she whispered, the touch of her Irish brogue returning as it did whenever she was upset or riled up, "I hear ye. What are ye all worked up about, child? Stop tinkerin' with that flute, and explain yourself!"

I peered through the keyhole at her neat blue skirts. This calmed me somewhat.

"Addie, I can't explain just now." I glanced back toward the window. The cloud of mist was swirling furiously around and over the windowsill. The flute tootled and trilled excitedly. "Just listen to me. I need you to keep Uncle Victor and Aunt Margaret busy for the next few minutes."

"But what d'ye mean, Lucy? I—"

I sighed impatiently, the sound of the mail-wagon bell growing more insistent.

"Addie, you must trust me! I'll explain it all to

you later, you have my word. But right now it could be a matter of life and death. . . ." I gulped at my own exaggeration, although it did indeed feel that important. "You just need to keep them distracted for a few minutes!"

I could almost see Addie on the other side of the door gripping the breakfast tray, glancing nervously down the stairs, biting her bottom lip.

"But, Lucy," she began, "I don't know. . . ."

"Just think of *something*!" I whispered. "Anything at all. *Please!*" If I could have opened the door and given her a shake, I would have.

There was a pause before I heard the crash of the tray on the stairs and Addie's voice calling out.

"Oh my stars! Oh good heavens! Mrs. Simmons, would ye look at what I've done now!" she shouted. I heard the scrambling of feet on the stairs, a confused jumble of angry voices.

I didn't wait an instant before dashing to the window. The misty vapor cascaded over the ledge and illuminated the side of the house below.

Of course! I couldn't believe I hadn't thought of it! Beneath my window hung one of Father's large, sturdy nets, which once strung between the masts of his great ship. This was another of Father's keepsakes from his sailing days, another bit of seafaring memorabilia that graced our home. The expanse of thick rope and fat knots had created a grid of footholds for Father's crewmen to scramble across. In the decade since Father left the high seas, the net had served as a curious kind of trellis, with wisteria, rather than sailors' feet, creeping up knot by knot toward the sky.

With scarcely a thought, I swung one leg over the ledge and searched with my foot for the top of the net. Encumbered and greatly exasperated by my full skirts, I hastily grabbed the hem with one hand and shamelessly shoved it into the waistband of my wide white bloomers.

In this way (much like a stuffed pillow), I made my way down the net, the scratchy rope chafing against my palms, my neat black button shoes slipping and sliding along the ropes. I had hardly a thought as to the safety of this escapade, for only the clanging of the mail-wagon bell spurred me on. As I neared the bottom, I felt the pins and needles of the mist at my feet and, chancing a look down, watched in amazement as the vapors actually curled back the wisteria vine, clearing a way for me. I watched the green curlicue tendrils loosen, uncoil, and creep aside as I placed my feet lower and lower.

Finally I jumped to the ground and ran toward the mailbox—a peculiar spectacle, I'm sure, what with my full skirts still jammed into my bloomers.

I waved at the postman, and, just as I hoped, he finally refrained from that infernal bell ringing long enough to jam a slim stack of letters into the box and gape at the strange sight of me barreling down the hill. Flustered and embarrassed, I'm sure, he left the mail, lifted the red flag, averted his eyes, cracked the reins across the back of the old horse, and was on his way.

As I flew toward the mailbox, I got a bit ahead of myself and stumbled. I tumbled forward and skidded across the dirt on my belly, leaving two great green streaks across my knees and a nasty tear along the seam of my bloomers. I was aware of my knees bleeding, but I scrambled to my feet and ran on.

Finally, out of breath and sweating like the dickens, I reached the box. I hurled myself at it, flipped the flag back into its resting position, and flung the little door open.

A stack of letters sat there waiting for me. I snatched them from the box and, still panting, began shuffling through them with shaking hands. An envelope from the village grocer, one from our family doctor, several more addressed to Uncle Victor from people I'd never heard of.

I slipped each of these to the bottom of the pile,

revealing the next and the next letter. As I fingered the last letter of the stack, I saw a shadow—a long, thin shadow—fall across the ground before me. I spun about to find myself face-to-face with my uncle.

I gasped and put my hands behind my back, shielding the precious letters from him.

"What do you think you're doing out here?" he snarled. His eyes were narrowed, and his expression was even more sinister than usual, what with the black-and-blue eye and his swollen, misshapen nose. He made a grab for my arm, and I quickly backed up, throwing him off balance. This infuriated him further.

"Give me those letters, missy," he hissed through clenched teeth. "It's bad enough you've disobeyed me by coming out of doors against my wishes. Don't make it worse by interfering with my mail, do you hear me?"

He made another lunge for me, and again I stepped back.

"I'm not interested in your mail," I said flatly. "I'm looking for my own mail. Mine or Mother's, which is none of your concern!" I was aware that I sounded most rebellious, and my shock at my own defiance seemed only to feed my behavior further. I was quite panicked, if the truth be known, and nearly out of control. Recklessly, I pressed on, Uncle

Victor's fury only adding to my insubordination. I set my jaw tightly and nodded at him with a *hmph* of determination.

"Why, you little hussy," he said, glaring at my bloomers, spitting the words. "How dare you leave the house like this? What are you trying to do—ruin my good name carrying on like a common street wench?"

I felt the color rise to my cheeks, and my shame further fueled my agitation. I hastily untucked my skirts, avoiding my uncle's eyes. He used that opportunity to fall upon me, wrenching the letters from my hands.

"No!" I shrieked and, shocking him as much as myself, I threw myself upon him, knocking the two of us to the ground.

Dear Lord, I knew at that point that I was in too deep to back off. Despite the fact that I realized no good would come from it, and that I could not hope to win out, I engaged him in a wrestling match, the two of us tumbling about trying to gain possession of those letters.

I stood finally, panting and gasping, filthy from head to toe, my hair wild and hanging in my eyes, staring at the stack of letters in his hands.

"Oh my good Lord, what are ye doin', Mr. Simmons?"

Addie grabbed me by the arm and yanked me to her. "What is goin' on here, for heaven's sake?" She looked wild, Addie did, staring openmouthed at the spectacle of the two of us. Behind her Aunt Margaret was lumbering across the lawn, huffing and puffing like a chubby locomotive, her skirts hiked up in her plump hands.

"What? What . . . happened?" Aunt Margaret gasped, out of breath, her eyes rolling about like those of a frightened cow.

Uncle Victor swiped at his hair, smoothing it back across his forehead.

"Disobeying me, she was!" he said. "Caught her running around out here in her *bloomers!*"

Aunt Margaret looked as though she might just faint dead away. I stuck out my chin even farther and stubbornly fought the tears that stung the backs of my eyes.

"'Tis true?" Addie asked, her voice more wrapped in that brogue than perhaps I'd ever heard it.

"No," I said, "it was just that I wanted to get the *mail!*" My words rushed out in a flurry, the last word, *mail,* stretching into an extended sort of wail. I refused to lower my eyes though, refused to give in to him. The tears rolled down my cheeks, but I checked the sob rising in my throat, gulping and clenching my teeth together tightly, holding my chin stubbornly high.

"In her *bloomers*?" asked Aunt Margaret, fanning her face, which by then was as flushed as mine. "Why wasn't she properly dressed?"

"Ask *her*!" shouted my uncle, who was himself red as a lobster; this along with the black and blue gave his angry face a purple cast, which made me think that perhaps he might just explode. It was an optimistic thought.

I shrugged in answer to their eyes, all three pairs of them fixed on me, Addie's gaze a mix of worry and confoundment, Aunt Margaret's one of shock and something between fear and confusion, Uncle Victor's full of pure fury.

"And not only *that*!" boomed Victor, waving the letters above his head. "She knocked me to the ground and tried to steal my mail!"

Aunt Margaret inhaled through pursed lips, shaking her head back and forth, staring at me as though I were some sort of circus freak or dangerous insect.

"I did not want to take *his* mail!" I shouted. "It was my *own* mail I was interested in. Mine and Mother's! And he won't even let me see what he's got there in his hands! He's the one who's stealing, I tell you!"

"Lucy," said Addie, "lower yer voice, lass." She pulled me in close and whispered into my hair. "This won't get ye anywhere, I tell ye. Calm down now. Hush!"

My heart was thundering, preventing me from breathing normally.

"Perhaps, if I may, Mr. Simmons . . . ," Addie began. "Seems to me that Miss Lucy just wanted t' look fer a letter from 'er auntie. That's understandable, sir, after all."

Uncle Victor's nostrils flared. "I'll thank you to stay out of this, Miss Clancy. And furthermore, if you don't start controlling your young charge here, I will see to it that that old coot of a lawyer has you dismissed and replaced by someone who can do the job expected of her! Imagine, a young lady, if I can go so far as to even *refer* to her as such, disobeying, running about indecently, and behaving like a hellion! That hardly reflects well on the job you're doing here, now does it? If you don't watch yourself, you'll be out on your heel, I promise you!"

"He's got my letter," I insisted. "I *know* he's got the letter."

"I'll hear none of it," said Aunt Margaret in a trembling voice, dabbing at her eyes with her hankie. "Of course he doesn't have any silly letter!"

Uncle Victor slipped the envelopes into the inside pocket of his coat.

"Now, take her inside, and get her cleaned up."

Addie nodded and took me by the arm, rather roughly, I might add. I suppose I couldn't blame her, being that my behavior had gotten her into trouble as well. I'm sure she was as shocked as any of them by my words and actions. I was quite shocked myself.

By the time we were halfway up the hill, my bravado had disappeared, and my anger had given way to despair. My defeat left me weak in the knees and sick to my stomach. I had ruined any chance of getting around Uncle Victor, had alienated Aunt Margaret, who, while not being especially kind to me, had always been at least somewhat sympathetic. I'd even put Addie, my sole supporter, in danger.

Back in the house Addie, tight-lipped and silent, ran a bath for me, the crease between her brows deepening.

Only Mr. Pugsley seemed his usual self, not at all put off by my dreadful appearance. He scurried around me, nudging me with his wet, flat nose; scouring me with rough kisses; wiggling his small curlicue tail.

I closed my eyes and lay back on my bed, rubbing his wriggling little body. A moment later

I heard Uncle Victor climbing the stairs. I sat bolt upright, my body suddenly electric. I could feel his anger prickle the air around me.

He stood in my doorway, a large brown burlap sack in his hands.

"The dog goes," he said. "I warned you, and you didn't pay me any heed."

"No!" I mumbled, tears choking off my words. I grabbed Mr. Pugsley and held him close. "No, you can't take my dog, I won't let you!"

He stalked toward me, the sack open in his hands.

"Put him in the bag," he said, his eyes black, still, and flat as a starless sky.

Trembling, I stood and stepped toward him, holding my small friend out in both hands.

"That's right," said Uncle Victor, "you'd do best to obey me this time."

I held the dog at arm's length, my bottom lip quivering, heart pounding. Uncle Victor thrust the bag toward me, holding it wide open, a gaping mouth ready to devour my little friend. I saw Addie out of the corner of my eye, standing on the stair, her hand covering her mouth, eyes shocked and shimmering.

I stepped forward and moved Mr. Pugsley closer to the bag. "It must be done," said Uncle Victor.

"The sooner you learn I don't make idle threats, the better!" He was warming to his hideous task, I could see. He chuckled and went on. "He won't survive the sea this time, I tell you!"

I threw myself forward and thrust Mr. Pugsley as far away from me as I could.

"Run, Mr. Pugsley," I screamed, "run!"

My uncle struck me across the face with the back of his hand. Addie screamed as I fell against the bed, but I sprang immediately back to my feet. My cheek stung wickedly, but my heart was dancing, for what I saw was the curlicue tail of my dear Mr. Pugsley bobbing rapidly down the stairs. Uncle Victor bolted after him, but not quickly enough. I rushed to the landing, grasping the doorframe with white knuckles. "Help," I whispered desperately, "please!"

The front door groaned and creaked and yawned, and with something quite like a sneeze, blew open.

The last thing I saw was Mr. Pugsley's backside hightailing it down the porch steps and across the yard, Father's ship's bell sounding his triumphant escape. He was safe, for now anyway. I backed up to the window, my eyes scouring the landscape for some sign of him.

I don't know how long I held my breath, but

when, in the distance, I saw the woman emerge from the bushes, I finally exhaled.

I watched, with a curious mix of relief and regret, as she scooped Mr. Pugsley up in her arms and disappeared back into the place, wherever it was, that she had come from.

11

It was a miserable day—the rest of the morning and afternoon following the incident at the mailbox and Mr. Pugsley's narrow escape—the worst day I'd had since the accident, without a doubt. It was true, I took some comfort in the hot bath Addie had drawn for me, the sudsy water providing some solace for my scraped knees and callused hands, the warmth of the water caressing my aching muscles. But even a soothing bath did little to ease my sorrow at losing Mr. Pugsley—the only consolation being that he was with the woman rather than drowned at the bottom of the sea in a mean burlap sack.

And as if losing Mr. Pugsley wasn't enough, there was Addie to contend with. After getting past her initial outrage and sympathy at my being struck by Uncle Victor, her mood slid into one of cool silence. I watched her anger and resentment coming my way via doors and drawers being shut a bit too powerfully, bed linens snapped and whipped into place with more gusto than required. When I spoke to her, her responses were clipped, and her eyes flashed darkly away from mine.

This was more than I could bear, and I spent much of the morning and the remainder of the afternoon trailing her from room to room like a frightened puppy, asking pointless questions, offering unnecessary help.

Finally she whirled about, facing me, and pointed a finger barely inches from my nose, an action so uncharacteristic that it stopped me there, dumbfounded.

"Ye can just stop yer followin' me room to room!" she sputtered. "It's best t' give me some time t' cool off, it is! I don't disagree that you've been unfairly and grievously treated. But when ye draw me into yer schemin' without me knowledge, and ye use me trust and concern for ye t' allow such wild carryin' on such as I've never seen, well . . . ye can't expect me t' be pleased about it, now can ye?"

She spun back around and stalked off down the hallway. Being taken off guard as I was, I opened my mouth and shut it several times, unable to find the words to respond. I skulked sheepishly after her, groping for something that might make her understand.

"But Addie, listen to me, please," I began. "It was the mail truck—the RFD—that I saw coming along the shore road. Don't you see, the postman may have left a letter from Aunt Prudence! If Uncle Victor had gotten there first . . ."

I swallowed back my tears at these words, for he had in fact gotten there, if not first, then certainly in time to spoil my plan.

"Don't you see, when I asked you to distract them, it was because I *had* to get to the box first!"

Addie rested the laundry basket on her hip and turned to face me again. "Well, will ye look at what came of it? Foolishly trustin' ye, I flung your mother's fine china down the stairs, what with thinkin' it was a matter o' life and death—that's how ye put it, if mem'ry serves me! And then, ye climb out a winda like some kind of a wild monkey and put up a chase in yer bloomers, fer heaven's sake!"

"But Addie," I began, remembering how my bedroom door had refused to budge, how the magical mist and Father's flute had led me to the window. How could I make her see that, at the time, it had seemed my only choice?

"I would've gone down the stairs and out the front way," I pleaded, "but the door to my room was stuck tight!"

"Oh, I see," said Addie, reaching out and opening my bedroom door with little more than the push of her finger. "So, this is the door 'twas stuck tight, was it?"

"Addie, *please*!" I crumbled down to the floor, my tearstained face in my hands, knees drawn up to my chin. I heard her sigh, watched her rest the basket of linens on the floor beside her. She knelt down and ran her hand across my hair.

Sighing again, giving up her anger, she pulled me gently to my feet and led me to my room. We sat together on the edge of the bed. I couldn't hope to explain everything to her, after all. How could I?

"Listen, darlin'," she said, her voice softer than before, "it's not that I blame you fer what you've done. Your Addie knows your heart is in the right place. And, Lucy, if you ever let yourself get wrapped up in these kinds of shenanigans, ye know I'll always take your side. But if it happens again, he'll have me sent away, d'ye realize that?"

"He can't," I said. "Father's will said—"

"Oh no, darlin', he can. If he can prove that I'm not doing my job, then he can have the court reconsider and send me off. And then what will become of ye, will you tell me that?"

She was right, of course. I hadn't allowed myself to think about that.

"But," I ventured, "if we don't find Aunt Prudence, we'll be stuck with them forever!"

Addie rubbed my back with her strong hands.

"Oh, go on now," she said softly. "Ye think yer old auntie would go off forever and never return? Of course not! We just have to wait, is all. We have to bide our time."

I let her comfort me, rocking back and forth beneath her touch, feeling the stonelike tension slowly drain away.

"Addie," I whispered, "do you believe in such a thing as a family curse?"

She froze, and her hands on my back stiffened. A shadow crept across her face, and her eyes shifted nervously.

"Where would ye get such a notion? Nonsense." She shook her head, as if to convince herself or to frighten off the thought. "There's no such thing as a curse, I say." Taking a deep breath, she placed her hands firmly on my shoulders. "Let's get back to the business at hand," she said. "Next time ye have an idea, ye tell me first. Do ye realize that if you'd told me about the mail wagon, I could've slipped out the back door with the gatherin' basket and been down to the box in a minute flat? We'd have had those letters tucked under the summer squash and the string beans, and yer uncle Victor would've been none the wiser. Do ye hear what I'm tellin' ye?"

I nodded slowly, realizing that my Addie was not as upset that I'd done the things I did as much as she was upset that I had jeopardized her place in my life. I threw my arms around her and let her hug me tight. Then she held me away at arm's length and looked me over.

"The captain would've been proud of yer spunk, miss," she said. She nodded and stood. "I have work to do. I'll try t' sneak ye a dinner tray later on."

She was gone in an instant, and I felt the first hint of relief I'd felt all day.

I was banished to my room, without so much as a book for entertainment, and the afternoon crawled. Day turned to evening, and Addie did manage to smuggle me a spot of tea and my favorite finger sandwiches of cold cheese and cucumbers. Later, I slept rather fitfully, this being the first night since the accident that my friend Mr. Pugsley hadn't shared my bed. Where had the woman taken him, I wondered, and did he miss me as well?

I passed the next several days in front of my window, searching the coast for any hint of Mr. Pugsley and the woman. I became more and more concerned, for there was nary a sign of them whatsoever, which caused me to think she'd disappeared with him for good.

Finally I was allowed back downstairs for meals. We were seated, all of us quite stiff and silent, around the dining room table. Addie was serving a cool summer soup and a platter of cold sliced meats and potato salad when we were interrupted by a loud knock at the door. My heart began to thump, as I continually hoped that news would surface regarding my aunt. Uncle Victor, perhaps thinking the same thing, raised an eyebrow, a dark cloud passing across his face.

"I'll get the door, then," said Addie, placing the platter on the table and turning on her heel. The food sat where it was as our eyes followed her to the entrance hall.

It was a woman's voice we heard, and Uncle Victor relaxed somewhat. Addie returned to the dining room, looking rather pale, it seemed to me.

"There's a lady here to see ye, sir," she began. "A Miss Maude, I believe she said. Says she runs a boardin' school for young ladies. Shall I send her away?"

My uncle Victor's eyebrows shot up, his eyes shining brightly, the corners of his mouth twitching.

"By all means *not*," he said, rising from the table. "Take the lunch away for now, Addie. We'll return to this later." He stood, swiped at his mouth with his napkin, and smoothed his shirt. "Well, don't leave our guest standing in the doorway like a common street vendor! Bring her into the parlor and then clear the table." He snapped his fingers at Addie, who immediately turned back toward the door.

"You," he whispered, pointing at me. "Tidy your hair! Gather yourself up! You are to wait here while I speak with Miss Maude. I'll call you when we're ready for you." He paused, shook a finger at me, and went on, his voice lowered. "Let me remind you that you had better try and behave like a lady and make a good impression!" He nodded impatiently at Aunt Margaret, who rather reluctantly removed her napkin from her lap and placed it on the table.

I followed them as they exited, as far as the dining room door, which my uncle slid closed behind him, just inches from my nose. I stood there, my ear pressed to the door, horrified. A boarding school? Was he going to send me away?

I heard the rustle of the woman's skirts brush the floor as Addie ushered her in, heard the sweet gush of my uncle's voice greeting her, leading her into the parlor, which was situated on the opposite side of the entrance hall.

I didn't dare slide back the dining room door even a smidgen, for fear of detection—especially in light of my recent carryings-on. I could certainly not risk another infraction. Instead I placed one of Mother's cut glass water tumblers against the door, the open end up against the wood as a kind of amplifier, the flat end against my ear. The result was a blurry kind of amplification that enabled me to at least follow snippets of their conversation.

After greetings were exchanged, the woman—who was, as far as I could tell, the headmistress—offered a description of her school. I strained to collect each word, or at least enough to piece together her meaning.

"... responding to your request for a governess ... displayed on the town bulletin board. . . ."

I gasped—a governess? What about Addie?

". . . Miss Maude's School of Etiquette . . . a finishing school for spirited young ladies . . . fine manners, homemaking skills . . . deportment and character refinement."

Uncle Victor immediately warmed to this line of thinking. His voice was louder, clearer than the rest.

"I absolutely agree with you," he boomed. "My niece underwent quite a distressing experience this past spring; perhaps you've heard?"

The woman must have mumbled a negative response, for Uncle Victor launched into his version of the accident.

"Out in a small skiff, the three of them—my brother, his wife, and Lucille. Now, I must tell you, in strictest confidence, of course, madam, that my brother was never one to exercise good judgment."

I was already seething, and the urge to burst through the door to correct him was almost more than I could bear. That, and the fact that he'd put out a summons for a governess! The only thing that held me back was the fact that an unruly outburst on my part would serve to validate my uncle's lies. I clenched my teeth, took a deep breath, and continued to listen.

"Rather than bring her in out of the storm, he capsized trying to rescue a local drunkard who had stranded himself out there on the water."

"Really?" the headmistress replied. "And I'm sure . . . a detrimental effect on the child."

"Well," said my uncle, in a tone that suggested he was letting the woman in on a secret, "the reality of the matter is that the girl has had to face the fact that her own father sacrificed the family in order to try and prove himself a hero—and as all self-serving plans tend to do, this one failed miserably."

"And the girl, your niece," said the schoolmistress. "How has she fared since the accident?"

"Not well, I'm afraid," said Uncle Victor, and then, as if his words might jeopardize his chances of shipping me off, he amended them. "Although, in an environment where there is more discipline, away from reminders of the past, where she could be in the company of other young women of her station, I believe she could turn things around rather nicely."

Perhaps the woman nodded, or murmured her agreement, and Uncle Victor strode toward the hallway, the sound of his approaching footsteps sending me back from the door, the glass hidden in the folds of my skirt.

"Addie," he called, in an unusually pleasant tone, "Addie, bring in the tea tray, would you? Miss Maude, have you had your lunch?"

She must have nodded. "Tea and scones, then, Addie," he called, and his steps took him back into the parlor.

I resumed my eavesdropping.

"A summer term, of course," she was saying, "could start as soon as tomorrow."

The opposite door swung open, the one that connected the kitchen to the dining room. I jumped at the sound, the glass slipping from my hand. It was only Addie, and I managed to catch the glass by lifting my skirts as a safety net.

"Ye keep liftin' those skirts and showin' your bloomers, and you'll be livin' at Miss Maude's School full-time," said Addie as she moved to the sideboard for the silver tea service.

I patted the folds of my skirts in place.

"Addie," I said, quite near tears at this point.

She came over to me. "Don't ye worry, lass," she whispered. "Barrister Hardy will need t' hear about this before any decision is made. It seems t' me that if yer in Miss Maude's care, then perhaps your aunt and uncle's duties will no longer be needed. This could be our way of getting rid of 'em for good!"

That was a new and novel thought. I could go off to Miss Maude's horrid school for a bit, Uncle Victor and Aunt Margaret would leave, and then I could return home!

"But Addie," I asked, "what about you?"

"'Tis not me that's important in all this. It's your welfare that matters. Besides, y'know I'd never leave ye!"

"But if they make you go too . . ."

"Not now," Addie whispered. "We'll figure it all out. Let me serve up the tea."

She took the tray into the kitchen, and as I

leaned against the door again it slid open, sending me sprawling on my face, the glass clattering to the floor.

Uncle Victor stared, his face nearly purple. Under his breath he hissed at me, "I thought I told you I expected you to make a good impression! This is an opportunity I will *not* allow you to spoil!"

I picked myself up and smoothed my skirts as well as my composure.

In a much louder, much more pleasant voice, he said, "Lucy dear, come into the parlor and meet Miss Maude."

I took a tentative step or two toward the parlor. Miss Maude was seated with her back to me. I took in her straight posture and full dark skirts spilling off each side of the chair. Her hair was wound tightly in a bun, this caught up in a no-nonsense hair net. Everything about her spoke of tidiness, restraint, and severity.

Uncle Victor took me by the elbow and propelled me into the parlor. I silently prayed for the magical mist to swirl about me, to perhaps close off the entrance to the room, or better yet, to open a space in the floor through which I could fall. I closed my eyes in the hope that I could conjure it up, hoping against hope that I might feel the pins and needles, that the electricity would course through me and rescue me as it had so many times before.

But there was nothing to save me, no magical mist to cloud my entrance.

I stood before my uncle on the Persian carpet, my eyes cast down at my feet.

"Miss Maude," said my uncle, "I'd like you to meet my niece, Lucille."

He squeezed my arm hard, a signal for me to raise my eyes. I looked up to find Miss Maude turning in her chair, no doubt to size me up.

When she rose to face me, I think I may have gasped.

I recognized those fine high cheekbones immediately, the straight nose, and, of course, the pale, sea-green eyes. My mouth hung open for a second or two before I recovered enough to maintain what I hoped was a normal, nonchalant expression.

"I am most pleased to make your acquaintance, Miss Lucille," she said, extending her hand toward me. Her tone was quite formal and serious, but there was a mischievous twinkle in her eye as she winked at me.

I took her hand and mumbled a response.

Uncle Victor led me to the sofa as Addie entered with the tea cart.

"Well," he said, smiling graciously, "shall we get on with it then?"

12

I cannot recall much of the conversation that followed—the details and arrangements seemed easily made, my fate quickly and succinctly sealed. I was just about nearly struck dumb, reeling between a feeling of giddy delight at going off with Miss Maude—after all, she had my dear friend Mr. Pugsley—and a feeling of utter dread; who *was* she really? I felt certain she was masquerading as the schoolmistress. And what if she was, in fact, a sea nymph—a siren? What was her purpose in taking me away? Only Addie, dear Addie, spoke up on my behalf, and in a rather forward and outspoken manner, I might add.

It was somewhere during Miss Maude's description of the required stitchery classes and the daily etiquette drill, all guaranteed to cultivate and refine the likes of me, that Addie piped up. She was clearing the tea, taking, I noticed, quite a bit longer than the task required. She paused, the tray suspended in her hands like a small drawbridge. "If I may be so bold as t' speak, sir," she began, "perhaps, in light of these plans, I can be of help to ye?"

Uncle Victor stared at her, his irritation blanketed in a tight smile, although it was not lost on me—nor on Addie, as I saw her face pale under his gaze.

"And what might that be, Miss Addelaide?" he asked.

Addie licked her lips and gripped the tray tightly.

"Well, sir, as I must run some errands in the village tomorrow, I thought I might serve as yer messenger, I might."

"Messenger, Miss Addelaide?" My uncle tapped his foot impatiently.

"Yes, sir . . . y'see, it seems to me that if Miss Lucy is leavin' us, well, then Barrister Hardy ought to know that our services are no longer required here; isn't that right?"

I almost choked on my scone, covering my mouth with my hand to prevent a spray of dry crumbs from shooting out onto the carpet. Addie's words had a similar effect on Uncle Victor and Aunt Margaret—Uncle Victor stretched and twisted his neck up like a giraffe, a red flush creeping from his collar up to his cheeks. Aunt Margaret gulped her tea a bit too quickly, resulting in a series of gurgly coughs and throat clearings. I expected to see the amber liquid bubble right up and spurt through her nose, but if it did, she covered it discreetly with her napkin.

I glanced at Miss Maude, who seemed to be enjoying the whole scene. When she saw me staring, she quickly rearranged her face into a more serious expression.

"B-b-but," Uncle Victor stuttered, "it isn't as if Lucille will be gone for good, is it, Miss Maude?" He looked to her for some encouragement.

"But of course not, Mr. Simmons," she said. "There are school holidays several times a year."

Addie pressed on. "So, as I was sayin', I can't imagine that fer just a few school holidays our services'll be needed here year-round. Perhaps then I should make arrangements t' close up the house?"

"Hogwash!" said Uncle Victor, anger flaring his

nostrils and popping the veins along his thin neck. "Who will tend to the house and grounds? We can't have the place in ruins, now can we?"

"But fer just a few days throughout the year, I can't see—"

"It is not your place to see," said my uncle acidly. I saw Addie swallow and step back, well aware, I'm sure, that her words would cost her dearly.

I believe Miss Maude noticed this as well, clearing her throat to cut the tension that sizzled in the air between them like electricity.

"Well," she said, in a calm, reasonable voice, "why don't we arrange for Lucille to return home on the weekends?"

"Yes!" barked Uncle Victor, leaning forward eagerly in his chair. "That was easily fixed, now wasn't it?" His voice had an "I told you so" tone to it.

Addie nodded, apparently relieved at the compromise, as was I, although her idea of sending the two of them off, their obligation fulfilled, was even more appealing. Even so, Miss Maude's suggestion calmed my nerves considerably. I could go off with her to find Mr. Pugsley, discover the reason for her masquerade, if that's what this was, and come back home to Addie. At least that's what I chose to believe. The fact was, I was nearly bursting with curiosity regarding the woman, and the mystery surrounding her filled my heart and mind with the kind of energy and sense of anticipation that one experiences in a stimulating, exciting life—much as I'd been used to in the richness of day-to-day living with Mother and Father. This feeling of curious expectation had been absent from my life ever since the accident, and up until this moment I hadn't realized how much I missed it. So, I chose to push aside my doubts about the woman—particularly the disturbing likeness I'd seen in our library painting—at least for the time being.

Father's steamer trunk was quickly hauled down from the attic and my belongings were stashed inside. I slipped my precious letter from Aunt Pru, extracted from beneath my mattress, and Father's flute into the bodice of my dress. In the few minutes that Addie and I had alone, we exchanged a number of assurances—I promising to behave in a manner that would have made Mother and Father proud, Addie that she would check the mail daily and come and visit as soon as she could get away. Addie railed on about my being sent off to a school no one had ever seen or heard about, and she promised to, one way or another, speak or write to Barrister Hardy about it. I, for my part, knowing what I did about the woman, urged Addie to wait until I had spent a week or so with "Miss Maude" before passing judgment. To this Addie reluctantly agreed, but only after carefully writing down the name and location of the school.

Uncle Victor, huffing, puffing, and straining under the weight of the trunk, nevertheless carried it out to Miss Maude's carriage single-handedly. After it was carefully placed on the rack at the back of the wagon, Miss Maude ushered me inside the coach, positioned herself on the seat up front, and took the reins in her hands. A tearful Addie rushed to the window against which I plastered my face (although I did not for a minute believe it was the cultured or refined thing to do), and we exchanged our good-byes. I was not as tearful as Addie, being anxious for the events of my life to move on.

Perhaps Miss Maude sensed my restlessness, for she wasted not a moment. Before I could reconsider (as if I had a choice), she gave the reins a snap, and we were off.

I gazed through the small square window at the sight of my house receding into the distance, Addie standing out in front watching us go. As we rounded the bend of the shore road, all that was visible were the turrets and the upstairs windows. I was suddenly overcome with panic along with an overwhelming sense of sadness.

The house seemed to watch me go, the large

upper-story windows, their shades halfway drawn like sleepy eyelids, gazing after me.

Through tears I leaned forward and blew a kiss toward my precious home. As my breath passed across my palm, it began to sparkle! I watched it whirl into a small glittering cloud, which drifted through the carriage window and up toward the house, expanding and spreading out in all directions. It floated up and around the porch, hovering over windows and slipping around doorways. The glittering cloud swelled and caressed each shingle and gutter, each brick and stone and timber, each nook and cranny, memorizing it for me. Finally it settled around the entire perimeter of the house and slowly, gradually, began to fade as though it had been absorbed into the very soul of the structure itself. I felt suddenly comforted, believing that some essential part of me had permeated the place, forever claiming it as my own.

As we approached the final bend that would separate me from the sight of the only home I had ever known, the ship's bell out by the porch clanged, marking my departure, and the window shades rolled up and back in tandem, blinking their farewell.

13

No sooner were we out of sight of the house than "Miss Maude" slowed the carriage to a stop, hopped off of the driver's seat, came around to the coach, and threw open the door. She stuck her head inside—I noticed that the tight bun was already loosened, and her hair fell freely about her shoulders, in stark contrast to the prim and formal dress she was wearing.

"Lucy, come on out and join me up front," she said, "where we can talk."

She offered her hand and helped me hop to the ground. In a matter of seconds I was seated beside her, sharing the reins, the ocean breeze blowing across my face.

"Miss Maude?" I asked. "Is that your name?"

She glanced my way. "It's a sort of family name—Maude, that is. But most call me Marni. Marni seemed an unlikely name for a proper schoolmistress, don't you think?"

I pondered this for a moment.

"So you're not really a schoolmistress?"

She tipped her head to the side a bit, as if considering the question.

"Not a schoolmistress, exactly," she said, "but you knew that right along, didn't you?"

I nodded, my mouth suddenly dry. I suppose a part of me wanted to believe that the story she'd told my uncle was true. I swallowed several times, trying to find my voice.

"Then if you're not a schoolmistress . . ."

"Why am I taking you off to school?" she asked, smiling broadly.

Again I nodded.

She stared off straight ahead for a moment before answering, her face growing serious.

"Well," she began, "it's true I plan on offering you an education, although not quite the education I described to your uncle."

"So you *are* a teacher then?"

"We are all teachers and all students, Lucy," she said. "But no, I'm not a teacher in the way that you think. I'm what I like to think of as a philanthropist."

I had heard that word before, I was sure.

"So . . . you give away a lot of money?"

She threw back her head and laughed. I felt my face flush with embarrassment, a fact that was not lost on her.

"Oh," she chuckled, patting my arm, "I know what you mean—and you are quite right. Philanthropists generally use their money to help people. I'm a philanthropist—but it is not *money* I use as a means to an end. Money is something I have very little of—and has been the cause of much grief and trouble in my family." Her face darkened for a moment, and she fingered the silver locket that hung at her throat. "I use other commodities to assist people—usually lost children with a variety of needs, none of which can be met by money."

"I thought that was why you took Mr. Pugsley," I said, "to help me—to help *him*. But I cannot understand how you know when or where you're needed. And where *is* Mr. Pugsley? When will I see him?" I paused to catch my breath. "And if we are not going to a school, then . . . where *are* we going?"

Her eyes widened at my rush of words, a smile pulling at the edges of her mouth.

"Lucy P. Simmons," she said, "an idle mind is certainly not one of your faults—I like that about you. But anyway . . . first, Mr. Pugsley, as you refer to him. I can assure you, he's been well cared for. The little imp is eagerly waiting for you back at my cottage. That is where we're going—to my cottage, which sits on the northern bay shore of Oxhead Bluffs."

I sat quietly, digesting this information. You see, our little peninsula, the one where our house sat, was on the south shore of the area that was called, by the locals anyway, Oxhead Bluffs. It was so named because of the way the land extended into the Atlantic in a pair of curved horn shapes, the whole landmass resembling the head of an ox. The two horns, so to speak, curved round to form a small, sheltered bay. Our home sat on the southern horn, ocean side. It seemed that Marni's cottage was situated on the northern horn, bay side. It was an area Father and I had sailed by many times.

"So," I ventured, "why are you taking me there, and what will you teach me?"

Marni stared off into the distance, her lips pursed. She took a moment before replying, as if gathering her thoughts.

"I was born with a gift," she began, "an uncanny talent for sensing trouble. This sort of sixth sense of mine has a way of leading me to people who are suffering somehow—usually children. Many times I am led to a place before the trouble even begins. That was the case with you, of course. I found myself here, and then there was the accident."

"You were there?" I gasped. "Wait—was it you who saved me? It was you, wasn't it?"

She paused, perhaps considering how much she should share. "You're here now and you're safe. That's what matters most." She patted my hand. "More often than not, once I'm drawn to a place, I proceed by instinct alone. A week ago I could not have predicted that I'd be here in this uncomfortable frock, in a borrowed carriage, masquerading as Miss Maude. But when the call comes, I've learned to trust and follow the impulse. That is how I am able to intercede at precisely the right time, in precisely the right way." A cloud passed slowly across her face, sharpening her strong features. "Only once has the gift failed me." The faraway look faded, and she smiled. "But that is in the past. And here we are."

"So, that is how you pulled me out of the water?" I knew I was fairly gushing, but I could not hold the words inside. "How you were on the path just in time to rescue Mr. Pugsley?"

"Yes," she said. "And this is also why I cannot tell you what I will teach you. I trust, as I hope you will, that I will be led to teach you whatever it is that will benefit you most, no matter how unlikely it may seem."

I nodded, thinking about the fact that her timing and her intervention so far had been impeccable. I also, however, contemplated the fact that she had been in the area at the time of the accident. The image of the painting of Ulysses, the Brute's words about the siren, the sea witch, flashed across my mind. A skeptical voice in my head suggested that perhaps her eagerness to help me might be a guilty reaction to her role as a siren in Father's accident. This I quickly pushed aside, hoping against hope that the voice in my head was wrong.

We rode silently for quite a while until we came to a small carriage house. Marni guided the horse into the yard and slowed to a stop.

"Time to return my neighbor Mr. Mathers's horse and carriage," she said, and in a moment or two had removed the mare's harness and tethered her to a hitching post set beneath the shade of a large tree. "From here we walk. It isn't too far, I assure you."

We walked along the shore road for what felt like miles, lugging my trunk between us. Finally we came to a small cottage clad in graying clapboard, wild roses tumbling over the lopsided, falling-down fence out in front. It sat overlooking the bay on a small rise of wild yellow-green grass.

"Here we are then," she said. We climbed the hill to the yard and looked out over the water. A ramshackle wooden set of stairs connected the house to an equally precarious-looking dock, where a good-sized boat was tied. Amazingly, from where we stood I could see clear across the bay, the turrets of my house jutting up above the pines that surrounded it like tall, dark soldiers. The sight of it, distant as it was, bolstered my spirits.

At that moment the front door swung open and Mr. Pugsley fairly flew toward me, his short, stumpy legs a blur of motion beneath his stocky little body. I was on my knees in an instant, and Mr. Pugsley covered me with sloppy kisses, grunting, snorting, and wheezing like a happy little pig.

"Mr. Pugsley," I repeated over and over, stroking him and showering him with kisses of my own. "Mr. Pugsley, I'm *so* glad to see you!" I tried, quite unsuccessfully, to fight back the tears that brimmed in my eyes, blurring my vision.

There was a sudden flurry of activity at the front door, and I glanced up, wiping my eyes with the back of my hand. The incongruous sight on the front steps jarred me, and I stared, bewildered, at the small group of children staring back at me. There were three of them: a tall, rangy black-haired boy, perhaps fourteen or fifteen years old, and another, smaller version, seven or eight years old, I'd guess. These two looked familiar to me, but try as I might, I could not recall when or where I had seen them. A small blond-haired girl of about four clung to the biggest boy's ragged trousers. I had never seen her before, of that much I was certain. But the other two . . . they triggered a vague memory that I just could not seem to place.

"Lucy, dear," Marni began, "stop gaping and say hello to Walter, George, and Annie Perkins."

Perkins . . . Perkins . . . the name rang a bell.

"Hello," I said, thrusting my hand toward them, "Pleased to make your acquai—"

The tall boy, Walter, interrupted me. "We've seen each other before, but I don't suppose you'd remember."

He made no move to take my hand, which I awkwardly dropped to my side. "Well, you do look familiar," I said apologetically, "but I can't quite recall where we might have met." I glanced at Marni, looking for help, but she was already making her way inside.

Walter stared at me rather coldly and said nothing. His little brother, George, looked away uncomfortably, and Annie, taking her cue from

Walter, stuck out her bottom lip at me in a most insolent manner. "And that's *our* dog," she said, bending over and pulling Mr. Pugsley toward her. Not wanting to contradict her, at least not yet, I held my tongue, understanding fully how quickly one could become attached to him. We could settle that later. I turned my attention back to Walter.

"Perhaps we met at the boat club?" I ventured, thinking of the many days Father had taken Mother and me over there for a fancy luncheon or a formal dinner.

Walter snorted. "Do we look like the sort who would belong to a *boat club*?" he asked.

I could feel the color rise to my cheeks. I'd insulted him, of course. It was obvious, from his shabby attire to his overgrown hair, that he was not of the same class as Father and Mother and me, that he wouldn't travel in the same circles. Feeling both embarrassed and defensive, I scoured my memory again. Where in the world had I seen them before? What was it about them that made me feel so uncomfortable?

Suddenly it came to me! It wasn't during the term before the accident, or even during the past academic *year*, for that matter. No, it had to have been more than a year ago that those two, Walter and his brother, George, had shown up at school.

I remembered the day now, how they arrived late, barefoot and dirty, and how they were ushered to the back of the one-room schoolhouse until Miss Randolph could decide what to do with them. Through hushed whispers I learned that they came from a dirt-poor fishing family, that their mother was dead. They stared about our classroom in a belligerent manner, daring anyone to meet their gaze. They were reputed to be unruly and dangerous. We steered clear of them, avoided their hostile stares, and for the most part pretended they weren't there.

As I recall, they didn't last long at school—they had both been placed with the youngest of students in the pre-primer class, and the older one, Walter, had bloodied a number of noses during recess time, successfully warding off the taunts of the other older boys.

"It was at school," I said softly. "You came to school for a while, didn't you?" This I offered in a most polite voice, hoping to feign ignorance regarding their school troubles. It was an awkward situation to be in, having to speak to someone you had previously chosen to ignore. I continued on, desperately trying to fill Walter's brooding silence. "I remember you didn't stay long. Did you transfer to another school?"

As soon as I spoke, I knew I'd made the situation even worse.

"Yes, Miss High and Mighty," he said sarcastically, "George and I transferred to a private prep school; didn't we, Georgie?"

George, apparently unaware of the subtleties of sarcasm, looked at his brother wide-eyed. "I don't remember that at all," George said, a concerned tone to his high-pitched voice. "I only remember the mean school. Is that the one you're talking about?" Walter ignored him, glaring at me instead.

Meanwhile, Marni, who appeared quite ignorant of my discomfort, had changed out of her schoolmarm dress and into a pair of denim overalls. Apparently no one else was the least surprised at the sight of her dressed in such an absurd way, busying herself with chores, bustling in and out of the house. I had never in my life seen a woman dressed like that! But, despite my surprise, what I really felt most was anger at her for leaving me there with Walter and, at the same time, shame.

I bit my lower lip, deciding what to do next. Walter had every right to be angry. He had been virtually invisible to me, like something unpleasant that washed ashore, something you didn't touch, something that the tide would eventually carry away. That was not going to be the case this time, I was sure. I took a deep breath and thrust my hand at Walter again. George looked seriously from one of us to the other.

"Walter," I said, "I'm very sorry. I was unkind to you. I didn't know any better then, is all; I just didn't think. . . ."

"Most people don't," said Walter. I could see he was softening a bit, but he still made no move to take my hand. I let my hand drop, but pressed on.

"I understand a lot more now than I did back then," I said, realizing as the words tumbled out that it was true. It was as though I'd left that other world completely behind. To my horror I felt tears sting the backs of my eyes and I fought to control the quivering of my bottom lip.

He avoided looking at me directly, a fact for which I was most grateful. "Marni told us you lost your parents," he said quietly.

"Yes," I replied. I blinked hard, raised my chin, and thrust my hand at him one last time. "Do you accept my apology or not?"

Walter took my hand then and, as if to ward off my tears, gave it a firm shake. Apparently taking their cue from their brother, George and Annie seemed to relax, their defensive expressions giving way to wide-eyed curiosity. Then they followed Walter in offering their hands.

"We lost our mother, too," Walter said. George kicked at the ground and looked down.

"I don't even remember her, though," said Annie. "She died when I was borned; right, Walter?" Walter nodded. I couldn't help but notice the tender way he placed his hand on her narrow shoulders, the almost imperceptible squeeze that he gave her.

"I'm very sorry," I said again, "for everything." Walter made a dismissive waving motion with his hand and looked away, his cheeks coloring.

"Why don't you have a look inside the cottage?" he asked, and before I could answer, he was leading the way in. I followed along, grateful for something to do besides talk.

The next half hour or so was spent settling me in. Marni ushered me throughout the cottage, pointing out this and that, George and Annie loping along behind us, watching my every move. The cottage itself was small and plain, the floors of wide-planked, pale pine, the walls whitewashed to a light sunny beige. There was little in the way of furnishings—a simple oak table, long and rectangular, in one corner of the room, surrounded by six odd chairs. At the opposite end of the room a stark, straight-backed bench resembling a church pew ran the length of the wall. It was not the furnishings, but rather the odd collections of peculiar objects and knickknacks that caught my eye. Large dried sea stars stood along the window ledges, their long bumpy arms reaching toward the wavy glass windowpanes. A huge conch shell claimed a spot in the center of the table, its weathered white armor curled around insides as delicate and pink as the skin of a baby.

And there were not only gifts from the sea adorning the place, but oddities that must have come from faraway, exotic places: a blood-red carpet splashed with jagged-edged geometric designs in gemstone shades of blue, green, gold, and purple. A silken shawl in sunset colors was draped around an overstuffed chair like a brazen ball gown, its fabric a tumble of paisley tied at the edges in long, exquisite golden fringe. A small corner cabinet held a collection of brilliant orbs of glass that sparkled and blinked in the sunlight like a group of wide-open, curious eyes.

Walter carried my trunk to a small room, and I followed him.

"This is it," he said, placing my trunk at the foot of my bed.

Annie shoved her way past me to the bed on the opposite side of the small room.

"This is *my* bed," she said petulantly, challenging

me to contradict her. She turned to Walter, her hands on her hips.

"I still don't see why I can't move to *your* room, yours and Georgie's."

"I've already told you the way things are done—the proper way, that is," Walter said. "It's girls with girls, boys with boys."

Annie sighed, folded her arms across her chest, and glared at me.

"I get to sleep with Toby!" she said.

"Toby?" I asked.

"The dog," said Walter. "Toby is what she named him."

"His name is Mr. Pugs—" I bit my tongue, I supposed, for the sake of getting along. I could see there would be no reasoning with her.

"All right," I said, "Mr. Pugs—the dog can sleep with you." For now, I added, silently, of course. We'd see, after all, who Mr. Pugsley himself preferred to sleep with.

Once I was settled, Marni took us outside, where my education was to begin, my first lesson involving the preparation of the evening meal.

"Chowder tonight," she said. "We'll need a couple of dozen clams."

She gave us each a large bucket, a short-handled rake-like tool, and a narrow pointed shovel.

She turned and looked me over, head to toe, a frown forming between her brows. "That frock will never do," she said. "Walter, bring her a pair of your overalls."

I felt myself flush at the very suggestion. I'd gotten into enough trouble tucking my skirts up into my bloomers. Imagine what Uncle Victor would say about me wearing boys' work clothes! Georgie snickered as Walter went back into the cottage.

"Go on inside," she told me, "and put on the overalls and a practical shirt." I hesitated on the step. Of course, I didn't own a practical shirt. What in the world would I have needed one for? Surmising as much, she nodded.

"Walter," she called again.

"Yes?" He stuck his head out the door.

"Lucy will need a shirt as well."

"Yes, ma'am," he said, casting George a sour look. I went inside and waited. In an instant he disappeared into his room and returned with a pair of well-worn overalls and a patched cotton work shirt.

"Here you are," he said, tossing the clothing my way, avoiding my eyes. I, for my part, grabbed the bundle of ragged clothing and turned on my heel toward my room.

I peeled off my dress and petticoats and slipped

self-consciously into Walter's clothing. I had to roll up the shirtsleeves and trouser cuffs several times in order for my hands and feet to emerge. The shirt felt amazingly soft, my body relaxing in the loose comfort of its folds. The overalls, too, had a cottony, worn feel as they brushed against my skin. I found that moving about in my new-old clothing was quite pleasant—the conservatively cut legs and arms afforded me a freedom of movement to which I was unaccustomed.

I stepped out onto the porch slowly, waiting for a comment about my transformation, but they were already walking toward the path, and I had to run to catch up. We were at the shore in no time. Marni rolled the legs of her overalls up over her shins and nodded at me to do the same. Walter and Annie and George were already knee deep in water, raking like crazy.

"Find the low-tide mark," Marni said to me, "and move just beyond it." I followed her into the water, cold even in midsummer.

"This is where we find the mature quahogs," she said, "and that's what we need for chowder. Back on shore, nestled in the sand, you find the smaller quahogs. Those are called littlenecks and cherrystones."

My first attempts at clamming were dreadful,

raking up nothing more than a few large stones and some seaweed. To my chagrin, this was the source of great amusement for the entire Perkins clan. I was much more successful on the mudflats, under Annie's direction, digging for steamers. First, we'd watch for a small squirt of water spurting up from the sand. That, Annie explained, was the clam spitting in anger before digging itself deeper. We'd watch for the spit, then dig with great diligence. It took a while to get the hang of it, but once I did, I found myself in much better stead with Annie. It seemed that she took credit for my limited success and saw my meager pail of clams as a tribute to her expertise.

Between us we came home with several dozen clams, which we cleaned and shucked and simmered in a great kettle of cream and onions and potatoes.

I could hardly recall a meal I'd enjoyed more.

Yet despite the contented, full feeling of the chowder in my belly, and the satisfaction I'd had in contributing to its preparation, my mood waned with the setting of the sun. The darkness brought along a certain strangeness, a solitary sadness that was different from the loneliness I'd experienced in my own home. My thoughts, filled with longing, turned to Mother and Father and to our days together that would be no more. I missed Addie, and wondered after my aunt Pru. Then my musings turned to bitter thoughts of Uncle Victor and Aunt Margaret.

I chose not to take part in the quiet games that Walter and George played together in the candlelight—cards and jacks and marbles—and did my best to ignore Annie's high-pitched lullabies that she lovingly sang to a dirty, worn rag doll. Instead I gazed out the window across the bay, hoping to catch a glimpse of a light in the window perhaps, a beacon from the house—*my* house—anything to reassure me that it still stood there waiting for my return. But there was only darkness.

I glanced away from the window finally, to find Marni staring at me intently, her book in her lap, a small pair of round spectacles on the tip of her nose. She removed her glasses, closed her book, and stood.

"Everyone to bed," she said. "Tomorrow will be an early day."

A cheer went up from the Perkins clan, and I found myself looking about, from one to the other. What were they so excited about?

"An early day, silly," said Annie, the *early* coming out more like *uh-ly*. "Don't you know what that means?"

I shook my head, a little tired of having a four-year-old explain everything to me. Marni turned my way, those pale green eyes of hers fairly boring through me. "An early day," she said carefully, "is a day when we sail."

Sail? I looked at her, my mouth agape. She looked away first, and went about clearing up the cards and the marbles and the jacks. "It's only fitting that a sea captain's daughter remain a good sailor."

To this I said nothing at all, for my voice was lost. I hadn't been out on the water since the accident. The thought of sailing again filled me with panic.

"But," I began, "I thought we would be studying tomorrow. . . ." My voice was small and tight and ready to crack. I hoped Walter hadn't noticed. I glanced about to find them all—Annie and Georgie and Walter—staring at me.

Marni stared at me as well, not unkindly, but rather with a determination and look of resolve that frightened me. She hesitated before she spoke, as if measuring her words.

"There are many means of studying, many avenues for learning." She nodded at the Perkins clan, and they lowered their eyes and went off to their rooms. Only Annie remained, half hidden behind the bedroom door, peeking around the doorframe. Marni approached me and leaned in close. Her peculiar eyes held mine, forbidding me to look away.

"Courage," she said softly. "I know it will take great courage for you to set foot on that boat."

A barrage of images tumbled through my mind—of Ulysses on the ship, his agonized face tilted skyward; of the siren in the water beckoning him; of Father and Mother, and the Brute, the water swallowing them up. And what about the curse? The Simmons family curse my aunt had referenced in her letter? It was one thing to pretend, ship's wheel in hand, in the safety of Father's chart room. It was another to actually venture on the treacherous waves. Marni waited and I gulped, squeezing my eyes shut, blocking out the images, fighting for control.

"Look at me, Lucy," she whispered. I felt her hand beneath my chin, raising my face to hers. I took a deep breath and opened my eyes. "It took great courage for your father to do what he did. Remember that."

I looked away, my uncle's words about the accident taunting me. How I'd wished, a hundred times, that Father *hadn't* been so brave; if he hadn't been courageous, he'd still be here. His courage wasn't something I was ready to give him credit for—not in the face of the tremendous loss it had caused me. Marni turned my face back toward her.

"Once you've learned courage," she said, "all of the other lessons are easy."

Hadn't I been courageous thus far? But would courage alone be enough to propel me aboard that boat?

Marni took my hands in hers, her grip amazingly strong.

"Courage is not about being unafraid," she said. "Courage has to do with moving forward in the face of fear. Do you understand?"

I nodded. I understood. I just hadn't accepted it. Not yet, anyway. She gave my hands one last squeeze and sent me off toward my room. I heard Annie skittering away from the door and diving under her covers. I undressed in the darkness and slipped into bed—a bed that felt nothing like my own bed back home.

What would happen to me out there on the water? I swallowed back my tears, fighting to stifle my crying. The bed shook with my silent sobs.

I became aware of something soft against my cheek. I caught my breath and reached out.

"Mr. Pugsley?" I whispered.

"No," came a voice. "It's me, Annie." Her small hand patted my face.

"Everything will be all right, Lucy," she whispered. The moonlight streaming in the window illuminated the top of her head, encircling her blond curls like a halo.

I sat up in bed, torn between surprise and embarrassment, touched and amazed that a child so young could recognize the quiet sounds of despair.

"Marni makes everything all right. You'll see." She sat on the edge of my bed and put her face right up next to mine, her eyes huge and round.

"You'll come on the boat with us," she said, nodding her head up and down, confirming the plan. "Yes, you will."

I nodded. "I'll go," I said, the sound of my own words making me tremble. I knew I was only pacifying her, masking my shame and my terror. "I'll go," I said again, desperately willing her to get off to bed.

"Do you promise?" she asked.

I swallowed and took a deep breath.

"Promise," I whispered, doubting even as I made the vow that I would actually be capable of carrying it out.

14

I spent a near sleepless night, tossing about in my unfamiliar bed, with thoughts of running off, stealing away home to Addie, where I could continue my quest to find Aunt Pru. Thoughts of escape and my fears tumbled together with the kind of wild, unrealistic plans that only seem reasonable in the darkest hours of the night. By morning I was thoroughly exhausted.

I lay still in bed, hoping against hope that they might leave me behind. Even the aroma of strong coffee, toasted brown bread, and sizzling eggs could not draw me from the cocoon of my bed.

"Breakfast!" Annie called brightly from the doorway. "Come on! Get up!"

I turned my back to her and drew the covers over my head. Mr. Pugsley jumped up and pawed at the lump of my shrouded body. He snuffled, snorted, and scratched with great enthusiasm, thinking my avoidance a new kind of game.

"She isn't gettin' up!" Annie called. I heard her steps retreat to the kitchen, felt Mr. Pugsley jump from the bed. The diminishing sound of his nails clicking on the floor, the snippets of breakfast conversation, and the clink of spoons and forks against plates left me feeling alone and bereft.

I pulled the blanket from my head, rolled over on my back, and stared at the ceiling. The cracks and peeling paint could have been a map—there a peninsula, there a continent, there an ocean. Somewhere out there, my aunt Pru.

A thought poked at the edges of my brain. I closed my eyes, tried to ignore it. But there it was. How could I ever find my aunt Pru out there in this great big world if I refused to sail?

My stomach turned over, recoiled, rumbled. Perhaps it was fear. Terror even. Or, I thought hopefully, perhaps the feeling of my stomach turning inside out was only hunger?

I willed myself out of bed, felt my feet hit the

floor, pulled my overalls up under my nightgown and threw the white garment off over my head. Quickly—my shirt! Quickly—my socks! Quickly, I headed toward the kitchen before this burst of courage left me. I turned back and grabbed Father's spyglass, hung it around my neck, and stopped once again. My flute! I swept it up from the dresser and placed it in the large pocket at my chest. I was rewarded with a flutter and tickle of air, a wisp of melody. *A la dee dah dah. . . .*

At the table there was no mention of my reluctance, no mention of my unkempt appearance due to my hasty preparation and lack of grooming. Marni slid a plate of eggs, sunny-side up, before me, followed by a stack of brown bread with butter and a cup of steaming coffee with cream. She nodded and smiled, gave my shoulder a squeeze. "A sailor needs a hearty breakfast!" she said.

Still, I pushed my breakfast around my plate until the dishes were cleared and stacked by the basin. At the last moment Marni scooped up a scone and an apple, which she pressed me to eat as we filed out the door. Georgie and Annie chattered all the way to the dock, their words buzzing around me like indecipherable bees. I was there and not there, half of me in the present, the other half desperately trying not to slide into the past.

"Lucy," Walter called. "You climb aboard with the others and help me with this line." He nodded to the rope anchoring the boat to the dock. "As I unwrap this end, you pull in the line, and I'll jump on."

There was no time to think about it. They were already ushering me aboard. As soon as he uncoiled the rope from the large brass cleat affixed to the dock, the boat began to move. I pulled in the line, forming large, neat loops as I'd seen Mother do. Oh, how I fought the image of Mother holding the line, the Brute yanking, and then . . .

Walter jumped aboard, grinning as he took the rope from my hands. "Good job, First Mate!" He thumped me on the back, and I blinked myself back into the present just in time to lower my head as the boom swung across.

From my seat at the stern I watched Walter approach the mainsail and Georgie grab the wheel, all under Marni's watchful eye. Mr. Pugsley hunkered down beside me with a resigned *hmpff* and lowered his head to his paws, surely remembering our previous trauma at sea. I managed to pull one white-knuckled hand from the side of the boat to pat his head, his resolute loyalty fortifying me. My eyes began to follow our little crew, anticipating each step in the process, the same practiced moves

Father had so skillfully executed time and again. There, they cleated off the halyard and pulled it taut. The bowline, secured. The luff, fed.

Walter coaxed me into helping with the jib, and as I pulled the canvas from the bag, I heard Father's voice, pointing out the head, the tack, and the clew. By the time the sails were hoisted, I was struck with a curious realization: never, since the day of the accident, had Father been more present to me than here on this boat, doing the things he loved to do.

"Ooh!" Georgie yelled, interrupting my daydream. "Look at that crazy bird!" He pointed to a cormorant doing acrobatics in the water. Annie squealed in delight at the sight of a playful seal poking its puppylike whiskered face out of the waves in greeting. Mr. Pugsley sat up and stared, perhaps mistaking the sea creature for a canine companion. His tail twitched and then tentatively wagged.

Before long Walter had me assisting him with the mainsail, and I let my hands automatically do the job Father had taught me so well. Walter nodded approvingly.

"Not bad. . . . Now I can see why they let you join the *boat club*," he teased.

I said nothing, not yet fully trusting my voice.

"How are you faring, Lucy P?" called Marni.

"Have you got your sea legs back?"

I nodded, determined, and my determination brought about an eventual calm. Walter seemed to sense it and smiled. Georgie took over, tacking this way and that, and Walter sat beside me.

"So," I asked, "how long have you stayed with Marni?"

He bent and stroked Mr. Pugsley's head. "We've been with her since last February."

Annie pushed between us.

"That was when we ran away," she said, "from our poppy."

I was aware of Marni in the background, listening but, it seemed to me, purposely staying out of the conversation. I looked back to Walter and noticed the edges of his lips twitch, saw his Adam's apple bob up and down. He glanced at me and then turned to his sister.

"We needed to find a new place to live, so we came here; right, Annie?"

Annie nodded, her dainty pink lips pursed like a small flower. "Uh-huh," she whispered. She looked at me with huge, solemn eyes. "Walter took us away so Poppy wouldn't hurt us anymore."

"He *hurt* you?" My heart leaped into my throat at the thought of a grown man hurting a little girl like Annie.

Walter stared out over the water. "Only when he had too much to drink," he said quietly. "But after Ma died, that was more often than not." He glanced at his sister. "Poppy couldn't help it, Annie; remember how I explained?"

She nodded and turned to me. "And it wasn't my fault, neither," she said in a soft voice. "Walter told me that, lots of times, and so did Marni. Right, Walter?"

"You're right about that," Walter said. "It wasn't your fault." Annie sat there nodding her head, trying, it seemed to me, to convince herself that her brother's words were true.

Walter looked at me, his face serious. "So, I ran off with them, and came here looking for work. Marni took us in. She'd lost her own son, years and years ago—she told us that. I like to think I fill his shoes, at least a little. That I can help her like she helps us. Our pop has been trying to snatch us back ever since, but we're not going back."

I almost told him again that I was sorry, but the dark shadow that had crept across his face, steeling his features, warned against it. I simply nodded, thinking what an odd bunch we were: Marni, the philanthropist who had lost a son (How? I wondered), and us—the Perkins kids and me, a peculiar group of misfits that she had somehow decided to save.

"Does your father know where you are?" I asked.

"He's seen us a couple of times," said Walter, "with Marni by the shore."

I saw Georgie stiffen, and watched Walter lay a hand on his shoulder. Georgie looked off across the bay, as if scanning the sea for any sign of his poppy. Apparently satisfied, he looked at me, his eyes wide. "He doesn't know where we live," he said, seemingly as much to convince himself as to convince me. Georgie turned to his brother. "He won't find us, right, Walter?"

"No," said Walter, with more conviction than I believe he felt, "he won't find us." I could see the tension slide off the little boy's face, a sight that endeared Walter to me then.

Marni took us out into the bay, along the whole inner rim of the oxhead horns in a southerly direction, almost to the opposite point where my own house sat. I watched it there—the house, that is—perched at the edge of the land, looking out to the east to the open sea. I wondered what Addie was doing at the moment, wondered if perhaps she was gazing on the water, thinking of me. Visions of squirrely Uncle Victor foraging around Father's desk and of Aunt Margaret's chubby fingers caressing Mother's fine china came to mind as well, but these I resolutely pushed aside.

We took turns using Father's spyglass. This enabled me to bring the house in more closely, to examine the shore that ran along the back side of the property.

It was while scanning the shoreline that I spotted something—just a slight motion at first, but enough to draw my eye back to the spot. I slowly turned the spyglass in a careful sweep, taking in again the area I'd just glimpsed. My heart raced, and I felt the color drain from my face. Sensing my distress, Mr. Pugsley bristled.

"What is it?" Walter asked. My mouth felt dry, the sight on the shore conjuring up the very memories I had fought hard to bury.

"What do you see?" he asked again.

I swallowed. "Just someone I recognize on the shore," I said, my voice sounding peculiar and hollow.

"You look like you've seen a ghost," Walter said, gently taking the spyglass from my hand, placing it against his eye, and squinting into the lens.

I felt a shadow fall across the two of us—not an actual shadow—more of a dark mood that descended as soon as Walter looked into the glass. He lowered the glass slowly and turned to Marni.

"Time to bring her around," he said, his voice

tight. Something in his tone immediately altered the atmosphere on the boat, the air around us charged with a nervous energy that almost tingled. Mr. Pugsley growled. The hair along his back stood up.

I watched Marni raise an eyebrow in Walter's direction, and without so much as a word, she changed course. In an effort that seemed well rehearsed, Walter and Georgie helped her, and before I knew it, the boat was sailing back due north, taking us away from my house, away from the shore, and away from the Brute.

Once our course was set, Walter glanced my way.

"How did you know it was him?" he asked.

"I remember him, of course," I replied, "since the day of the accid—" I paused, confused. "How do *you* know him?" I asked.

Walter looked at me as though I was rather dim-witted.

"How do *I* know him?" he repeated, his voice wrapped in a laugh that held no humor whatever. "That man on the shore is my father!"

"Your *father*?"

I was incredulous. The Brute was their poppy, the man who had hurt them, the very same man who was responsible for the accident!

It all made sense now. No wonder the Brute had been chasing after Marni—he knew she had his children. And Mr. Pugsley—that explained why Annie claimed he was her dog; he had, after all, belonged to the Brute to begin with. I had just never imagined him, with his wild hair and unshaven face, having a family, never dreamed he had children. All of this I took in as I slumped, my back against the side of the boat.

"Lucy," said Walter, impatience sneaking into his voice, "I still don't understand how you recognized him."

I shook my head, not feeling quite able to put it all into words. I glanced at Annie, who upon overhearing us began clinging to Marni's trousers, her thumb in her mouth.

"George," Marni called, "George, take over here, would you?"

He nodded, and in an instant Marni lifted Annie in her arms.

"It's all right, Annie," Marni said. "No one's going to hurt you. You're safe here. I won't let him take you." Annie wrapped her legs around Marni's waist and buried her head in her shoulder. Marni rubbed her back and glanced over at us.

"So, now you see that it was more than simple coincidence that brought you all together. Your lives have been intertwined by fate."

"But I still don't understand," Walter said again. Georgie looked from one of us to the other, the worried crease forming between his brows giving him the look of a little old man.

"You see," Marni said to Walter, "your father was stranded out on the water this past spring during a fierce squall. He was not . . . well . . . in good condition at the time. Captain Simmons, being a seasoned waterman, managed to rescue your father. But, in the process, the Simmonses' boat capsized. Lucy and Mr. Pugsley managed to escape. The Simmonses—the captain and his wife—were not so lucky."

Walter hung his head for a moment and then looked up at me. "Your father and mother drowned trying to save Poppy?"

I nodded. He looked away for a moment and when he looked back at me, his face was clouded.

"I'm sorry," he whispered. "Your father must have been a great man."

I nodded again, not only in response to the words he spoke, but to the unspoken words as well—acknowledging that the better man had certainly not won out.

We sailed on in silence, each of us lost in our own thoughts. Marni did not interfere, but rather focused her energies on overseeing the workings of the sails, thus giving us time to let the peculiar circumstances of our relationship sink in.

It occurred to me that my joining the group had put us all at a disadvantage. It would be critical that the Brute *never* see us together, the Perkins children and me, for all it would take for him to recapture his children would be to spot me at home on a weekend visit and follow me back to Marni's cottage.

Still, he hadn't seen me with them yet, and I longed for a visit home to see what progress Addie might have made. Although I was grateful to Marni for many things, the weekend, I thought, couldn't come quickly enough.

15

The days that passed between our small voyage and my weekend visit home did not inch by as I had expected they would. The fact is our days fairly dashed by, filled with study—although study unlike any I had ever undertaken back in school with Miss Randolph.

No, this was a much more lively education: mornings spent immersed in ancient leather-bound books, the dry powdery pages smelling faintly of salt and cedar, filled with the lore and legends of the sea.

It was the tales of piracy that captured Georgie's

attention, and I must admit, mine as well. A far cry from the days when the Perkins brothers were relegated to the back of the country schoolhouse, Georgie had become something of an orator, with a gift for dramatic reading.

"Grace O'Malley," he boomed, gesturing with one hand and holding open the book with the other, "was a pirate, a warrior, and a gambler, feared by the men of her day! The first in a line of fearsome Irish women pirates," he proclaimed, "she left home at a tender age, returning with her abundant mane of red curls shorn into a masculine style. She captained many a ship along the western shores of Ireland, wreaking havoc wherever she sailed!"

Annie and I applauded. "I'll bet she looked like *you*!" Annie chirped, scooping up my curls and tucking them behind my head. Grace O'Malley, I thought, a woman with roots in the seafaring life. With that thought, something rose and thrilled inside of me. With my curls tucked neatly, I hopped up onto a chair and assumed the role. On my perch I launched into my hardy repertoire of sea chanteys, with Georgie and Annie jumping in on the refrains. For my finale I played Father's flute with many a flourish, ending, as always, with *"Ah la dee dah dah, a la dee dah dee!"* Even Walter clapped vigorously and whistled in a rowdy manner. I bowed deeply. "To Grace O'Malley!" I shouted, raising a fist in the air.

Only Marni sat, stock-still, her features turned to stone.

"What is it?" I asked. The room fell silent.

"It may be great fun to glorify piracy," she said. "But the lawlessness and brutality they practice has affected generations of decent people! This I know firsthand!" She fingered the silver locket at her throat.

Her tone silenced us, discouraging comment or question. Another of her many mysteries. But before we had a chance to wonder too deeply, her nimble fingers worked two lengths of rope, one red and one blue, and we practiced tying nautical knots of various kinds. "Walter," she said, "you and Lucy work on the carrick bend; Georgie and Annie, the icicle hitch."

We tied and untied, cooperating, giving and taking, securing more than rope and twine. A comfortable familiarity began to enfold us, finger to finger, knot to knot. Then there were maps and charts to read, and geography books to study, all of this embellished by Marni's tales of travel. This, of course, brought me around to thoughts of Aunt Pru, which I set aside as best I could, waiting,

waiting, for the weekend to come.

And come it did. Another trek to Mr. Mathers's to borrow the horse and buggy, and Marni and I were on our way. We left at dawn, the sun nothing more than a fuzzy pink-orange line floating over the ocean, the milky outline of the moon still visible through the brightening blue sky. Annie and Georgie hung in the doorway, begging to come along, Annie's mouth pulled into a petulant pout. Walter waved, and corralled them back inside.

By eight o'clock we had arrived. Marni (or Miss Maude, as I had to keep reminding myself) spoke briefly to Uncle Victor about my progress, all her comments of a very general nature—"a satisfactory adjustment," "a conscientious pupil"—comments to which Uncle Victor nodded distractedly, apparently eager to address the more important issue of my return to school.

"And you'll come back for her, when?" he asked, leaning forward, his head cocked to one side.

"I will send the buggy for her on Sunday afternoon," Marni replied in her Miss Maude voice, all business; the only hint of her other self was the discreet little squeeze she gave me on the arm on her way out the door. In seconds I was fairly flying up the stairs to Addie, who was patiently waiting on the landing.

I threw myself into her embrace, remembering all at once the warmth of her arms, the clean, soapy smell of her hands, the crisp feel of her starched dress. We walked, arm in arm, up to my room and sat on the bed.

"Aye, I've missed ye somethin' awful!" she said, holding me at arm's length and looking me over, as if searching for something she might have overlooked—something that might have changed in the week I'd been gone.

"I missed you too," I said, feeling a little guilty over all of the time I'd spent so completely engaged in my other life with Marni and the Perkinses.

"So, is it a grand school yer at there?" asked Addie. "And how are ye bein' treated?"

"Fine," I replied. "I'm getting on fine there." I wasn't sure how much to tell Addie, at least right away. I was far more interested in affairs here at home.

I lowered my voice to a whisper. "Have you been checking the mail?" I asked.

Addie nodded, the edges of her mouth turned down.

"Aye, I've checked it—every day, in fact—but the RFD never comes. I fear your uncle's suspended the service here, and that after all of the captain's efforts to bring it out here in the first place!" She made tsk sounds with her tongue, shaking her head. "He's been to town twice since you've gone, checkin' the postal office, I imagine."

My heart fell, even though I had suspected as much. Addie wiped her hands on her apron and looked away.

"Addie," I said, "there's something else, isn't there?"

She bit her bottom lip and nodded.

"What is it?" I asked, my heart quickening.

She shook her head. "I'm not sure how to put it in words," she said, "or quite what t' make of it, even."

"What?" I said. "Please, Addie, do tell me!"

She paused, considering. "There's been quite some strange goin's-on in yer absence, is all."

"What kind of goings-on?" I asked.

Again Addie paused and avoided my eyes. She seemed almost embarrassed, uncertain about what she was about to say, reluctant to begin. Her hesitation began to alarm me.

"Addie, what is it? Tell me, please!"

"'Tis probably just me imagination, although I never b'fore in me life have seen such as I've seen, and I cannot think of a reason why me imagination should begin to run wild at this particular place in time."

"Addie?"

She stood. "Never ye mind," she said, "'Tis a bit of nonsense is all."

That's when I knew—it was the magic!

"So, you've noticed?" I said. "The magic, I mean. And did it help you too?"

She turned toward me, her eyes flashing.

"What was it ye said, then?" she asked. "Did I hear ye right?"

"The sparkling cloud," I replied. "That *is* what you saw, isn't it?" I feared for a moment that I'd said too much.

Addie's eyes grew large and round. "So ye've seen it too, then?" she asked, sitting back down on the edge of the bed.

I nodded. "It kept me out of trouble—many times since Uncle Victor and Aunt Margaret came."

Addie's mouth dropped open. "And nary a word t' me about it?" There was a trace of hurt, or maybe it was resentment, in her voice.

"It's not that I didn't *want* to tell you," I began. "But I was very perplexed. I thought, at first, that perhaps I was seeing things. And if I'd told you, would you have believed me?"

Addie shrugged a little. "I s'ppose ye have a point," she said. "Well, let me tell ye how it all began." I propped up my pillows on the bed and leaned back and patted the space beside me for Addie. She shook her head, positioning herself instead so that she could see out the door as she spoke.

"Yer uncle Victor," she said, in a hushed voice, "he began to carry on in a manner I found quite suspicious. He went off t' town, as I mentioned—t' the postal office, I suppose—and upon returnin' he'd hole up in the captain's lib'ry fer the whole of the afternoon. There he'd sit all hunched up over the desk, cursin' and swearin' at the fountain pen in 'is hand. It appeared he was working on correspondence of some kind."

Correspondence—that could mean he'd heard from my aunt Pru!

As though reading my mind, Addie nodded. "Of course, ye know what I took to thinkin'—that he'd gotten a letter from Prudence! So, I made it my business t' find out, though 'twas no easy task, I'll tell ye—"

"What did you d—"

"I'm gettin' t' that," she said, pushing aside my anxiousness with a bit of impatience.

"I waited fer the two o' them—yer aunt and uncle, that is—till they went into town the next day. When they were gone, I took meself into the library." Addie leaned forward and peered out into the hallway. Apparently satisfied that we could continue our talk undetected, she went on, her voice barely above a whisper.

"I went t' the desk, I did, and set about looking fer the letter, if that's what 'twas—but I found the desk was locked up tight! Being that they'd gone to town, I was struck with the notion that perhaps I could find the key, or give the lock a little poke with a tool o' some kind—not t' break it, mind ye, but t' pop the lock open."

I nodded vigorously, anxious for her to continue.

"Well, I searched fer the key, everywhere I could think of, 'cludin' under the carpets, behind the draperies—I'm ashamed to say I even looked about in yer uncle's chambers, something I'd never dreamed o' doin', in the interest of my employer's privacy, but in this case—"

"I know, I know," I said. "Then what happened?"

"An hour I searched, an hour at least, but I didn't find any key, of course—he most likely took it with him in 'is pocket. So I went on t' me next plan, which was t' open the drawer some other way."

"So, how did you do it?" I asked.

"Well," Addie said, "I looked about the kitchen for somethin' of the right size and shape—and I settled on the rug beater."

The rug beater? It was the size of a tennis racket! "How in the world would you use the rug beater?" I asked.

Addie made an exasperated huffing sound. "Surely I didn't intend t' use the entire rug beater," she said. "I bent one of the wires back so's it could be slipped into the lock."

"Did it work?" I asked, nearly breathless with excitement.

"No," said Addie, "and not only did it not work, but the bent wire got stuck in the lock! And no sooner was it stuck in there than I see yer aunt and yer uncle makin' their way up the path!"

"Oh no!" I said, my heart pounding as though it was I standing beside the desk with the rug beater hanging there as evidence. "Did they catch you?"

"Well," said Addie, suddenly, it seemed to me, taking a certain pleasure in keeping me in suspense, "'tis the strangest part o' the whole story. There I was, yankin' at the rug beater with every bit o' might I could muster, and workin' meself up into quite a sweat, I might add, when I see this sparklin' cloud. At first I blinked, thinkin' 'twas me eyes and me nerves, playing tricks on me. But, no, it swirled about the rug beater, liftin' the handle and turnin' it round, like the hand of a benevolent ghost or spirit, and just like that I hear the lock turnin' over in the barrel, and the desk drawer bursts open!"

She paused for a moment, perhaps reliving her

surprise at such an occurrence. "Well, I tell ye, time runnin' out as 'twas, I didn't stop to marvel too much—yer aunt and uncle were already makin' their way up the front walk. So, I rifled through the drawers like a common thief, and let me tell ye what I found."

"What?" I asked, barely able to contain myself.

"A letter from your aunt Pru is what I found."

"Where is—"

"Now hold yer horses," she said. "I said I *found* it—but I wasn't fool enough to *take* it!"

My heart dropped for a moment, but my curiosity quickly pushed past my disappointment. "Well, what did it *say* then?" I asked, leaning forward, eager for her to continue.

"Not to get yer hopes up, lass," Addie began. "'Twas nothing in it that would help ye—just some greetings and inquiries fer yer mum, and words explainin' how she'd been so far off down under that she neither expected t' receive or t' send out mail in any kind o' timely way. And she asked after your father and you. Said she continued to collect clues, whatever that meant. Said she had tales of piracy to tell!"

I slumped back on the pillows, my disappointment threatening to erupt in tears. I was unreasonably angry at Addie, furious that she had risked so much to discover so little.

"So after all that, you didn't find out *anything*?"

Addie looked at me. "Now, is that what I said? No, I found somethin' all right. 'Twas but a minute or so left; I could hear them bickerin' like they do out on the front porch. So's quickly as I could manage, I went through the drawers. 'Twas a whole tablet of paper there, covered in a peculiar script. I took a piece of it, without thinkin' really—it just seemed that with so many pages, he'd hardly be missin' a single sheet. I slipped it into my pocket and made haste to go. I shut the drawers, all of 'em, I did, but that sparklin' mist reappeared, I tell ye, and drew the bottom drawer open again! I struggled with it fer a moment, fearin' I'd be discovered, but the mist wouldn't allow the drawer to close! I took another look in the drawer and what did I see but a letter from Barrister Hardy! I read it with me heart in me throat, listenin' to them right out there on the porch."

"The letter?" I said. "What did it say?"

Addie took a deep breath, confirming my fears that the letter did not bear good news for me.

"It said that the barrister was returning t' England t' care for his ailin' mother. That someone else, a Judge Forester, would be overseeing yer affairs from now on."

That seemed a terrible blow. I'd always felt that if things got bad enough with Uncle Victor and Aunt Margaret, at least I'd have a sympathetic ear, a fair and objective ally in Barrister Hardy. Now, with him gone . . .

Addie went on. "Well, what with yer aunt and uncle halfway in the door, I gave the drawer a push and, thank the Lord, finally it closed. The mist swirled about and the rug beater floated—it actually *floated*—out of the lock, and I heard a bit of a click, which of course was the sound o' the drawers lockin' themselves back up. By the time yer aunt and uncle came in, I was on me way to me chambers, the rug beater in me hand, requirin' a bit of time to calm me nerves, which I must say are still more than a little shaky."

Addie paused as if to further calm herself, and then pulled a paper from her pocket. "'Tis this I took from the drawer," she said quietly. The page was covered in script, the same three words over and over:

Miss Prudence Simmons Miss Prudence Simmons
Miss Prudence Simmons Miss Prudence Simmons

I stared at the page, not grasping its meaning. "But what—"

Addie interrupted. "'Tis what he's spendin' his days doin'," she said, her eyes blazing. "Sittin' there in the captain's chair with yer auntie's letter before him—this I know 'cause I've managed to get in there with the excuse of needin' t' clean this, or t' polish that, and I've stolen a look over his shoulder, I have. He's practicin,' I tell ye—he's practicin' at copyin' yer auntie's hand!"

I gasped as the realization hit me.

"But why?" I began. "What for?"

Addie took my hand in hers and stared at me, hard.

"I can't be sure, lass," she whispered. "But that's what I mean to be findin' out!"

16

Sunday afternoon was upon us quickly, and it seemed we had barely finished with the afternoon meal when the clip-clop of Mr. Mathers's mare could be heard on the drive outside. I patted my mouth with my napkin, backed away from the table, and prepared to take my leave.

Even though I was prepared—Addie and I had my few necessary belongings packed—my departure this time was more uncomfortable than the last. There was something disturbing in Uncle Victor's manner—nothing as harsh as the time he'd struck me, or, for that matter, his words not as biting and sharp as they had been before I left with Marni. No. Harsh words or even the back of his hand would have meant business as usual. But something had changed.

All weekend there had been a distractedness about him, as though his primary goal was not to vex me and remind me of our family faults—mine and Father's, mostly. Rather, he spent most of his time holed away in Father's study.

And neither did Aunt Margaret seem herself. Each and every time I was in her company, her eyes would dart nervously from my gaze and an anxious flush would creep up her neck and across her cheeks. As if to distract us from this, she spoke incessantly in a flustered, rambling way about nothing at all—that is, until Uncle Victor silenced her with some harsh demand or chore that would occupy her elsewhere.

And finally there was the visit from a man Addie and I had never seen before. He was a person of some means—this was obvious from the look of his well-tailored clothing, the large gold pocket watch that dangled by his side, and his expertly trimmed and waxed mustache, which curled above his upper lip like the wings of an extravagantly plumed black bird. It was clear to me that the man disliked my uncle but was working hard at concealing this.

His words and gestures spoke of congeniality, but his smile was snakelike, and his eyes—small black eyes—were unrelenting and cold. I watched the man pull back slightly as my uncle laid a hand on his shoulder and led him into the library. Uncle Victor was carrying a ledger of some kind; the other man, a well-oiled leather satchel.

As he shook hands and readily accepted a brandy and a cigar, it seemed to me that the man *wanted something*—and he was willing to flatter and patronize my uncle in order to get it.

All of this was lost on my uncle Victor, who seemed to revel in the man's slippery overtures, returning each with another ingratiating gesture of his own. Had my uncle been a decent person, I might have felt sorry at the deception taking place, but Uncle Victor being who he was, I felt only disgust.

All of this flashed through my mind again as I gathered my things to leave. There was a rap on the door, and in a moment Addie led a man, an older gentleman, into the front hallway.

"Marcus Mathers," he announced. "Miss Mar—" He made a big show of clearing his throat. "Excuse me," he said. "As I was saying, Miss *Maude* sent me for the young lady."

I was deeply disappointed that Marni herself

had not returned for me. My uncle barely raised an eyebrow, simply nodded toward my things. "Well, let's get the wagon loaded," he said, although he made no move to help the man.

Mr. Mathers lugged my traveling bag out the door, and I was pleased to see that the horse and carriage were familiar.

Addie and I tagged along behind. Uncle Victor followed us out, moving quickly, rushing us along, edging in beside Mr. Mathers and giving my bag an impatient shove. It was clear that he was eager to get back inside to his brandy and cigar.

"Mr. Mathers," my uncle said, "as to my niece's subsequent visit . . . next weekend will be most difficult for us—I have quite a lot of important business to attend to. We'll need to make it two weeks, or, better yet, three. That will bring us to the very end of the summer, a fitting time for a visit before the fall term."

I watched Addie beside him, her mouth narrowing into a thin line, the color rushing to her cheeks. She opened and shut her mouth several times as if to protest, but no words came.

Mr. Mathers shrugged, his long, jowly face devoid of any expression. "I can't see Miss M— Maude finding a problem in that, can you, Miss Lucy?"

I shook my head and squeezed Addie's hand. Maybe it was better that I was away until the problem, whatever it was, blew over. For there was, undeniably, a feeling in the air of some change that was being kept from us, that promised to bring no good. Addie hustled me toward the carriage. "I'll be watchin' 'im like a hawk, I will," she whispered in my ear. "Don't ye be worryin'!"

Uncle Victor turned to go, but then hesitated, perhaps thinking that propriety required some kind of a farewell.

"Ah yes, dear," he said, gazing just to the side of me in order to avoid my eyes, "you will be missed, of course." To this I said nothing at all, and Mr. Mathers's eyes swept questioningly from Uncle Victor to me and back again.

I saw my uncle tense under his gaze. He was working quite hard at controlling his anger at me for not responding in kind to his deceptive overture. He swallowed and curled his mouth into a smile that barely masked the look of distaste beneath it.

"Until then," he said, and to my great discomfort he embraced me—if you call a rigid, cold sort of hug an embrace. I stood stiff as one of the stately pines surrounding the house and did my best to tolerate this deceitful show, put on for Mr. Mathers's benefit.

Mr. Mathers opened the carriage door and helped

me in. I was delighted to see Georgie there, looking so tiny alone in the back of the buggy. He sat with his arms folded, clutching himself, kicking his skinny legs against the bottom of the seat. He smiled shyly at me, and shimmied over to give me more room. I heard the soft clicking sound that Mr. Mathers made to get the mare moving, this and a gentle snap of the reins. We lurched forward, and I peered out the window at Addie, and at my beloved home.

Again I was overcome with a feeling of great loss. I sniffled for a bit, wiping my bleary eyes and runny nose with my hankie. Suddenly there was nothing I wanted more than for Mother's arms to hold me, for Father's hands on my shoulder. An awkward period of silence followed.

It was Georgie, finally, who spoke.

"I wanted to see your big grand house," he said seriously. "I think that's why Marni let me come along."

"Uh-huh," I said, my voice still thick and coated with tears.

"What's the matter?" he said anxiously. "You don't want to come back with us?"

I shook my head. "That isn't it." Even to me it sounded unconvincing. Georgie looked disappointed, a shadow falling across his small, fine features.

"Well," he said, frowning, "your house wasn't *that* grand."

I shrugged, understanding that he was punishing me for my lack of enthusiasm.

Georgie gnawed at the edge of his tiny half-moon of a thumbnail. "And, with such a grand house," he mumbled, "I don't see why Marni needs to help you anyway."

I placed my hand lightly on his shoulder. "Georgie?"

He continued to kick the seat, peering straight ahead as though he hadn't heard me. "My house may look grand, but it's not the house itself, you see. It was being there, so happy, with my mother and father, and Addie. All of that was lost when the accident happened. So, you see, it's good for me to be with you. You've all been kind to me, and you've helped me spend my days being productive rather than sulking about pitying myself."

I overlooked Georgie's incessant kicking as best I could and went on.

"And I'm sure you can understand how having a grand house hardly makes up for losing a mother or a father." The tapping stopped, and Georgie looked up at me, his bottom lip stuck out, transforming his face into a dark-haired version of his sister Annie's. He nodded and the tension lifted. We rode along like that, in silence, for some time before the carriage jerked to a stop.

"Whoa, Gert," said Mr. Mathers to his mare. "Easy now."

I leaned forward and glanced out the window to determine what was causing the delay.

"What in God's name could be so important that you practically throw yourself in front of my wagon?" asked Mr. Mathers.

From the angle of the window, it was impossible to see whom he was addressing. I craned my neck and peered out. All I could see was a pair of old boots and some denim trousers, obviously belonging to a rather large man. Georgie and I vied for position at the window, pointlessly, as the man was standing outside of our view.

"I saw you talking to her!" bellowed the man. "I want you to tell me where she lives!"

I watched Georgie's face go white, and I grabbed hold of him as he shrank from the window and melted into the space beside me. It was clear that he recognized his father's voice, and his reaction to it told me more about their relationship than Walter had disclosed.

"Down here, Georgie," I whispered. I lifted my skirts by straightening my legs at the knees and shoved Georgie into the space underneath. I lowered my legs, allowing my skirts to drape over him. I nudged him this way and that until he was mostly covered, and then dragged my traveling bag closer, hopefully concealing any sign of him whatever. I sat still, every muscle in my body tensed, waiting to see what might happen next.

"I don't know who you're talking about," said Mr. Mathers evenly. "Now step aside, we have a journey ahead of us."

"The sea hag!" shouted the Brute. "I saw her at your place! That witch has my youngsters, do you understand me? And I mean to get them back!"

Mr. Mathers made that clicking noise again, and the carriage moved a bit before lurching to a stop.

"Get your hands off of that harness," Mr. Mathers said firmly. "I don't want to have to run you off the road, but if you persist, I shall have no choice."

"That woman stole my children," the Brute bellowed, "and you know where they are!"

I felt Georgie grab hold of my ankle, his fingers pressing painfully into my skin.

"You'll be safe, Georgie," I whispered, but my heart raced wildly.

"You're talking nonsense," said Mr. Mathers. "You have no business here with me. Now let us pass!"

"You're lying!" screamed the Brute. I heard Georgie gasp, could feel him cowering beneath my legs.

"I won't let him take you," I said, meaning it with all my heart, terrified that I might not be able to follow through on my promise.

"Be off with you!" said Mr. Mathers. I heard the snap of the reins and felt the carriage move forward.

"Who have you got in that fancy carriage, anyway? Is it her—the sea nymph?"

I watched out the window and, to my horror, saw the Brute lunge toward the carriage door, felt the impact of his large hands against it. The door swung crazily open as Mr. Mathers drove old Gert forward. I thought of reaching for the door and pulling it shut, but feared that any motion on my part might reveal the little stowaway. Instead I clung to the edge of the seat and concentrated on keeping my legs rigid, thus preventing Georgie from tumbling over and out the door.

The Brute ran alongside us, his wild eyes bulging, his chest heaving. He grasped the edge of the doorframe and leaped toward us, managing to get a foothold along the bottom edge of the rig. I hammered at his grimy fingers and dug my fingernails into his flesh. He yelled and cursed like a banshee but somehow held on. The carriage pitched to the right and to the left, an attempt by Mr. Mathers, I'm sure, to disengage the Brute. Holding my breath, I pried at his thick fingers, my heart threatening to explode. "She isn't here!" I screamed, and realizing my mistake, added, "Whoever it is you're looking for."

There was a terrible moment when I thought for sure that Georgie and I would be tossed out onto the road, the instant that Mr. Mathers nearly took us into a ditch. The carriage tipped dangerously to the left, sending me and Georgie, still hanging on to my skirts for dear life, sliding across the seat and toward the open door. The Brute clung on, but the crazy tilt of the carriage caused him to lose his footing. He was flung backward and landed sprawled out across the grass. We went crashing on down the road, the carriage door flapping and banging against the side of the buggy like a window shutter in a hurricane. Finally, when the Brute was far out of sight, Mr. Mathers slowed to a halt and jumped from the buggy seat.

I found myself gasping for breath, my muscles weak and trembly.

"Where's the boy?" asked Mr. Mathers, his dark eyes darting frantically around the inside of the carriage.

"Here," I whispered, relaxing my legs and moving them to the side. Georgie's head emerged, and he glanced up, my skirts encircling his face like a ruffled bonnet.

Mr. Mathers's shoulders slumped in relief. "We've left him far, far behind," he said. "It's all over. You're safe, now." Georgie didn't move.

"There's not a chance of him catching up with us. Probably got the wind knocked clear out of him. Gert and I'll get you two back in no time at all, and I surely am not about to tell him where I've left you. Come on then, Georgie, it's safe to come out."

For now, I thought uneasily. He's safe *for now*. But it was obvious that the Brute was getting closer to finding his children.

Georgie crept out from under my skirts and wedged himself between me and the wall of the carriage. He seemed quite frail suddenly—his dark hair messed and standing out in all directions, his skinny little arms wrapped protectively around himself. He seemed to me to be as young and vulnerable as a baby bird.

Satisfied that we were settled, Mr. Mathers secured the carriage door and set off, still driving the old mare a bit more strenuously than I'm sure she was used to.

When we rolled to a stop, I expected that we'd

be on the road in front of Marni's cottage; however, this was not the case. Mr. Mathers jumped off the buggy seat and led the horse along a narrow path that wound away from the shore, and eventually out behind Marni's cottage.

The three of them—Marni, Walter, and Annie—met us there, a look of concern flashing between them when they saw us coming in the back way.

Mr. Mathers opened the door, and Georgie and I climbed out, the sunlight causing us to squint after the dark of the carriage. My legs felt weak, the muscles quivery, and I thought for a moment that they might give way. Mr. Mathers took Marni aside, and the two of them stood shoulder to shoulder, their backs to us.

"Out on the shore road," I could hear Mr. Mathers saying quietly. "It seems he spied you out at my place. That's why I came in the back way," he went on, still whispering. "Thought it'd be impossible for him to catch up to us. Just the same . . ."

"I do appreciate it, Marcus," Marni said softly. "The next time I come by, it will be under the cover of evening, I promise."

✳

The weeks that followed had an unspoken tension surrounding them that colored every hour of the day and night. We spent most days out on the boat, honing our sailing skills—this, I'm sure, in part so that if the Brute ventured near the cottage, there would be no sign of us.

Evenings were spent inside, the windows covered with shades of dark-blue oilcloth, blocking out the ocean breezes that usually kept us cool and comfortable—this because there seemed to be eyes everywhere, watching from the shadows. In every dim nook and dark place, the Brute took shape in our imaginations, invading the safe haven that Marni had made for us. We listened anxiously, tensing at every snapping branch, every rustling in the night. Annie took to sucking her thumb, Georgie to nibbling his nails, and Walter to pacing the floor. Even Mr. Pugsley felt it, as evidenced by his restlessness when awake, and during sleep by disturbing dreams in which his short legs would mercilessly twitch and jerk, and he would yelp and cringe quite piteously.

We made a show of spending our twilight hours reading quietly, although I, for one, had to read and reread the same page many times before moving on. As the evening stretched out before us, we often set aside our books and spoke of the dreams that we held most dear to our hearts. Walter dreamed of sailing a grand ship of his own, traveling the world over. Annie and Georgie spoke of all of us staying together forever as a family, with plenty of distance between us and their father, the Brute. And you know my dream, the one I shared with Addie—that we would someday find Aunt Pru, and oust Uncle Victor and Aunt Margaret from the house so that it would be wholly ours again. Marni listened quietly, never voicing a dream of her own, fingering her silver locket, each moment seemingly fulfilling enough in and of itself.

It was on one such evening that Annie and Georgie had gone off to bed, reluctantly as usual. Both of them had become light, restless sleepers, the Brute robbing them of their dreams even in his absence. The night was drenched in humidity, the air still and flat in an uneasy, overbearing way. It would only be a matter of time before the thunder rolled across the bay, before the sky was ripped open by lightning.

We sat together in silence—Marni and Walter and I—the tick of the ancient mantel clock marking the passing of seconds.

"Maybe I should take them somewhere else," said Walter, his voice rough, his eyes distant. My heart lurched, and I suddenly realized how much I didn't want that to happen.

Marni rocked in her chair and gazed at him. "I

believe, Walter," she said, "that sometimes it isn't in the frantic doing or the fixing, but rather in the patience, the quiet, in which our answers are revealed to us."

"So I should just wait here until he finds us and drags us off?" Walter asked, straining to control his voice so as not to awaken the little ones. "Is *that* what you think I should do?"

"Marni won't let him hurt you!" I blurted. "Will you, Marni?" I turned to Walter. "And when things get especially bad, there's sometimes . . ." I hesitated. "Magic," I said quietly.

Walter rolled his eyes. I had, of course, never spoken of the magic, of the sparkling mist, partly because since my departure from home it had seemed less real to me. If the truth be known, I could almost believe that it had never really happened. But now, I found that I needed to believe it.

Marni turned to Walter.

"Some things are meant to happen and some things not. I've learned to listen and to yield to whatever wisdom or revelation comes. I wait until I am sure of the voice inside me—and then I trust it completely. I feel that you are right to stay on here. But you must listen to the voice of your own heart."

Walter looked disappointed, as was I. I wanted her to insist that he stay, to assure him that everything would be all right, that she would protect all of us forever. The clock ticked on.

Marni continued rocking in her chair, the gentle squeak at counterpoint with the ticking of the clock.

"Walter," she said quietly.

He looked up.

"The only thing I ask is that you wait until that inner voice is clear and true—to wait until the discord in your mind narrows to a single voice. Until that happens, any decision you make may be the wrong one. Do you understand?"

He nodded slowly. "I'll wait until I can think it through. I promise I will."

Suddenly, Mr. Pugsley growled, the fur on his back raised in a sharp ridge.

We sat for a second, still as stones, the grasp of terror holding us in our seats. Then Marni rose slowly, calmly, and began walking toward the door.

17

The seconds slowed to a crawl as Marni slipped back the latch, laid her hand on the knob, and turned it slowly. Walter and I sat, too frozen in fear to question or to protest. I not only felt, but *heard* my heart throbbing, the blood pulsing in my ears. I was hot and cold all at once, my insides racing out of control.

We heard the barrel of the doorknob click and disengage the lock. In less than a heartbeat the door flew open with such force that it swung back and crashed against the house, shaking the little cottage to its very foundation.

I covered my face with my hands. Though I could block out the sight before me, I could do nothing to block out the sound. I shall never forget the words I heard in that moment—they were not the words I expected at all.

"Thank God I found ye, lass!"

I dropped my hands and jumped to my feet. It was Addie, dear Addie! She looked frightful—her hair wild with the humidity, her chest heaving, the bodice of her dress drenched in sweat, the hem of her skirt and her shoes covered in dust.

"Addie!" I yelled, throwing myself at her. So relieved was I that it was she and not the Brute, I scarcely stopped to realize something must be terribly wrong.

"Listen, now will ye! We haven't much time!" she said.

Marni walked over and laid a hand on Addie's shoulder.

"Welcome, Miss Addie," she said quietly. "Come and sit for a moment and tell us, whatever it is."

By now Annie and Georgie were standing in their bedroom doorways, concern widening their eyes and furrowing their brows.

"Come, sit down," Marni said again, taking Addie by the arm.

Addie didn't move.

"There'll be no time fer that, I tell ye! Miss Lucy has got to get home, and if I can beg your indulgence, miss, I'd like ye to come along as well. There's trouble back at the house, there is. I slipped away as soon as I was able, stole the neighbor's horse to get here, and as 'tis, I fear it might be too late! And, to top it off, the feisty mare ran off, leaving us no way back!"

"What is it?" I asked, a nauseous feeling snaking around my gut. "Tell us, please."

"It's yer uncle," Addie said. "I figured out what he's been up to, I did. I told ye how he's been workin' night and day in the lib'ry, and I showed ye how he'd been dippin' the pen in ink and practicin' yer auntie's hand—well, now I know why."

She paused, out of breath, and pushed a few damp curls off of her face. The first rumblings of thunder sounded in the distance like a drumroll before a proclamation, and we all inadvertently paused until it stilled.

"Go on," I said, my mouth filling with saliva, a hot acid feeling rising from my stomach.

Addie looked at me, her eyes blazing. She took a deep breath and continued.

"He's claimed to have gotten a letter from yer aunt Prudence, he has. Even showed it t' the judge, so he says—the judge who took over fer the good barrister.

The letter—and I've managed t' get a glimpse of it, I have—it says she got word of the tragic passing of her dear brother and sister-in-law. That she sends her condolences and her love t' ye, but that her plans will not be allowin' a return t' the States, that her study and her work make it impossible fer her t' come and care for ye, or fer the house. That she relinquishes her claim t' any part of it and asks the court t' put yer aunt and uncle in charge."

I sank back into my chair, certain I would be sick. Walter came and knelt beside me, Annie, Georgie, and even Mr. Pugsley following his cue.

I swallowed and shook my head.

"It's a lie," I said, "all of it. He wrote that letter himself!"

Addie nodded, her lips in a tight, angry line. "Course he did," she said. "He wrote the letter, signed 'er name, and placed it in the envelope from the letter he stole from ye that day out at the mailbox, that's what he did!"

"Well," said Walter, jumping to his feet, his eyes indignant and black as coals, "I say we go back there and tell the judge what he did!" Annie and Georgie nodded in agreement, although I doubted they understood much more than their brother's loyalty and sense of justice, which echoed in his tone of voice. Marni looked at Addie. "There's more, isn't there?" she asked.

"Ye bet there is!" said Addie. "Goin' t' the judge—'twas the first thing I thought of. I went t' town and I went t' 'is office, I did. He wouldn't see me, but I refused to take my leave! I must admit, I made somethin' of a scene. Finally he ordered one of his associates t' usher me out, and in quite an ungentlemanly way, I might add. But I got a glimpse of 'im—the judge, that is—when his office door opened."

She paused, shaking her head at the memory.

"The judge," she said finally, leveling her stare at me. "Judge Forester. He's the very same dandy of a man that came callin' the last time ye were home."

I gasped. "The man with the fancy mustache?"

"The very same," said Addie. "And that isn't all."

"What else?" I asked, dreading the answer.

Addie took a deep breath. "It seems the court has already considered the matter. They've appointed yer uncle as yer sole guardian, with what they call the power of attorney over the estate. What it means is that Victor can do what he likes in yer regard and in regard t' the house."

"But, how can . . . ," I stammered.

"I'm afraid ye still haven't heard the worst of it," Addie said, reaching for my hand. She took a deep breath. "Given that yer uncle's taken charge o' things, he claims he's goin' t'sell the house!"

I felt as though I'd been punched and had the wind knocked clear out of me. Georgie gasped, his small eyes wide, remembering, I'm sure, the grand house he'd been so impressed with. Walter paced the floor, and Annie, looking from one of us to the other, seemed about to cry, her thumb planted securely in her mouth. The air suddenly became even more oppressive, so thick with tension and humidity that it pressed on my chest until I thought I might be crushed by it. A clap of thunder, closer than before, shattered the moment.

Walter spoke up, his words angry and clipped. "Anyone can see that this is ridiculous! At least it seems as though the court should stop the sale of the house until there's a hearing or something. And what about Lucy? Even if the house is sold, shouldn't that money be hers?"

Addie nodded. "I asked Victor that, I did. Told me he'd already had a hearing, that of course Miss Lucy'd receive the proceeds, but that he'd be the manager of the funds until she reached her eighteenth birthday. Said he and Margaret would be movin' back to Ohio and that Lucy'd be put up at the school here permanently. And then he threatened t' dismiss me on the spot fer puttin' my nose where it didn't belong."

Marni rubbed at her chin. "How can I help?" she asked, her eyes filled with a distant look, as if seeing something none of the rest of us could see.

"Well, as I was sayin'," Addie went on, "he said 'twas all done, there was nothin' else t' discuss. But I simply cannot abide by it. What in heaven's name will stop 'im from goin' off t' Ohio, or t' God knows where, with Miss Lucy's money and then disappearin' altogether, slippery as he is, and never showin' her money *or* his weaselly face again? What's t' stop 'im, I ask ye? He has no concern fer the child, I can vouch fer that! And, if all of it weren't bad enough, he claims t' have a buyer fer the house!"

It was almost too much for me to bear. I sank even deeper into the chair, into the embrace of its wide, soft arms.

"It's surprising that he was able to arrange it all so very quickly," said Marni.

Addie shook her head. "Well, 'tis not so surprisin' once ye hear the rest of it—the worst of it, in fact," said Addie. "The buyer of the house, 'tis none other than the fine judge himself—crooked as the Piscataqua River, I tell ye! And, if I overheard what I thought I did, he'll be comin' by this very evenin' with the paperwork in hand. So, you see, if we're t' stop 'im, we must be goin'—it might already be too late!"

Marni looked from one of us to the other, from Walter to Georgie, and then to Annie. "Walter," she said, "will you stay here with Georgie and Annie?" He began to protest and she raised her hand, silencing him. She paused for a moment, that distant look in her eyes again. She stood like that—still and silent, her eyes remote, her gaze far away. We all stood quietly, afraid, I suppose, of intruding on whatever vision held those sea-green eyes of hers.

"You're right, Walter," she said finally. "We will all go together. Quickly now, get whatever things you'll need—your clothing, your books—Annie, take your doll, and your box of special things."

We all did exactly as we were told. I can tell you that my hands shook, and that I felt cold despite the heat, much like a person feels when in the grip of a fever. Even Walter's face was white as snow. We knew, all of us, that something was about to happen. None of us dared to question what exactly it was. Instead we concentrated on gathering our things, stuffing them into bags and satchels. My spyglass I hung around my neck, my flute tucked in my pocket against my chest. No one mentioned the fact that we knew we would not be returning to the cottage, to this safe haven. No one spoke the words, but we knew—even Mr. Pugsley, who scurried around the rooms nose to floor, sniffing out a farewell memory.

As I gathered my most precious possessions, I do remember feeling that, in spite of the troubles that seemed insurmountable, I was suddenly very much alive, fully present in the moment.

We took less than we left behind, and as we followed Marni out the door, I paused, taking one last look at the sea stars on the windowsills, the glass orbs twinkling on the shelf.

Marni turned. "Lucy," she said, gesturing toward the door. "It's time."

I shuddered then and, surrounded by everyone in the world that I loved (except, of course, my aunt Pru), I followed Marni out into the night.

18

The first thing I noticed as we made our way down to the shore road was the moon, huge and pale and white, hanging over the water just as it had the first night I'd laid eyes on her—on Marni, that is. The last time when it hung over the water, it had shone clear and cool as a pearl, but this time it hovered over the sea shrouded in mist that blurred its edges and encircled it like a pale, fuzzy halo. It lit a dim bluish path ahead of us down to the road.

We walked swiftly and silently, like a small band of devoted warriors committed to our mission. It wasn't long before the thunder rumbled closer and we were sprinkled by the first tentative drops of rain. When a bolt of lightning struck, sizzling and sharp, searing the sky and slicing the sea, we all jumped in unison like a trained formation of soldiers. Chins down, the rain at our backs, we quickened our steps, the impending storm lending an even greater urgency to our campaign.

In minutes we reached Mr. Mathers's. Marni rapped on the door, the sound lost in the clapping of thunder.

"Marcus," she called. "Marcus, come quickly!"

There was a scuffling sound, a rattling of the lock before a rather rumpled Marcus Mathers opened the door.

"Good Lord, Marni, what on earth . . . ," he mumbled as he ushered us in out of the rain.

"It's like I told you," she answered, "although not quite the emergency I had expected. We need to get us all back to Lucy's place, and as quickly as we can. Could we borrow the carriage—"

"Don't say another word," he said, pulling on an old jacket that hung on a hook near the door. "Let's get Gert harnessed up, and I'll drive you over."

We ran out behind him, all the way to the barn. He lit a gas lamp, and the sleepy mare looked mournfully in our direction, sensing, I think, that her quiet evening tucked in the warm, dry barn was over.

Walter helped harness her up, her tail flicking nervously with each clap of thunder.

"All right," said Mr. Mathers, "climb in." He hustled us into the carriage—Marni, Annie on Addie's lap, Georgie, and me—and took his place with Walter up front. He clicked his tongue, and we were off.

By the time we were back on the shore road, the storm had grown dramatically worse. The rain beat down in sheets on the roof of the carriage, and the wind pummeled its sides. When lightning struck, it lit the inside of the carriage, making our faces ghostly and white, flash freezing our expressions for a moment. Annie whimpered and snuggled closer to me. Georgie perched on the edge of his seat, his white-knuckled fingers gripping the ledge, peering out the window. Addie and Marni sat silently, Marni deep in thought and Addie, it seemed to me, just plain exhausted.

A sudden jolt tossed us against one another and sent Georgie sprawling onto the floor. Annie howled. We jerked to a stop, the impact toppling her beside her brother. Addie helped her up, as Georgie scrambled to the window. Mr. Pugsley began to growl. Marni absently patted his back to settle him down. Her eyes, though, were not on Annie, nor were they on the dog.

"Stay here," she said as she swung the door open and climbed out.

The sounds of the storm poured in, bringing with it a rush of wind and rain, as well as the sound of angry voices.

"Get out of the way! We'll run you over if we have to!"

It was Walter's voice. I knew then, and so did Georgie. I could see it on his small, pinched face.

"It's him again," Georgie said, his voice twisted. "It's him."

Addie looked questioningly at him. "Who, darlin'? Who are ye so afraid of?"

Annie continued to cry. "We shouldn't have come out here. Now he's gone and found us. Is he going to take us away?"

"*Who*, child?" Addie asked, a hint of impatience mixing with her concern.

"The Brute," I whispered, more to myself than to anyone else. The sound of angry voices rose and fell with the howling of the wind and the rain. Thunder boomed. It was impossible to make out their words. My mind was reeling—had he grabbed Walter? Would he burst into the carriage at any moment and steal away Annie and Georgie as well?

I looked desperately about for some way to defend my friends. But it was hopeless.

"Lucy," said Addie, "who is causing this delay? Why is everyone so terribly frightened?"

"It's their father," I answered, panic creeping into my voice. "The Brute. The man Father saved."

Understanding flashed across Addie's face, then fury.

"Hasn't he caused us all enough trouble?" Addie asked, her voice tight. "I'll not have any more of it!"

She pointed at Georgie and Annie. "The two of ye stay where ye are!" she ordered as she pushed her way out of the carriage. Mr. Pugsley and I scrambled out behind her.

Lightning flashed every other second, illuminating the scene in a series of horrifying images: The Brute knocking old Mr. Mathers to the ground. Addie cradling Marcus's head in her lap. Walter shoving his father off balance. The Brute lunging for him. Marni between Walter and the Brute. The Brute swinging wildly. Pugsley snapping at the Brute's legs. The Brute kicking him hard.

In the midst of this, Georgie and Annie screamed from the window for everyone to stop.

It was Annie's voice that captured the Brute's attention, that briefly distracted him from pummeling everyone in reach.

He stopped for a moment, his eyes wild.

"Lucy, get back in the carriage," Marni directed. I inched back, but just couldn't bear to get inside. Not with Walter, Addie, and Marni facing him there. With Addie's help, Mr. Mathers struggled to his feet.

The Brute took a step closer to Marni. "You witch," he snarled. "Give me back my young'uns! Walter! George! Annie! Come with me!"

Marni held him there with her eyes, her chin lifted defiantly. "You'll *not* have the children," she said. "You cannot do them any good. They're better off with me, and you know it."

His face twisted into a gruesome, contorted mask. A growl erupted from his lips.

"They're my offspring, and I have every right to have 'em!" He stepped back suddenly and swung around to face Walter. "Tell her!" he shouted. "Tell her you belong with me!" The begging sound that crept into his voice showed me he was not only afraid of Marni, but of his own children's revulsion— afraid of the reflection of himself he saw in their eyes. Walter must have heard it as well and, gaining courage, stood his ground.

Marni spoke up. "You'll *not* have them," she repeated. "Now, step aside and let us pass. Addie, help Marcus into the carriage."

She helped the old man, and Walter stepped around his father to the carriage, measuring the distance between them with his eyes. The Brute turned his attention to Annie, who was watching, whimpering, from the open window. "Stop that blubberin'," he said, and raised the back of his hand toward her. She stopped immediately, her eyes wide with terror, her mouth trembling.

"Don't you *ever* raise a hand to her again!" Walter spat out the words and lunged at his father, though the Brute was twice his weight and a full head taller.

In that moment I forgot about the house, the forged letter, my uncle's betrayal. All that mattered was Walter.

Mr. Pugsley, clearly still in pain and limping slightly, barked furiously at the two of them wrestling on the ground. I started toward them, thinking only of helping my friend. Addie grabbed hold of my arm and we had a struggle of our own, my eyes fixed on Walter and the Brute.

For a moment Walter had the advantage, as, in his surprise, the Brute was momentarily stunned. Walter pinned him to the ground, but not for long. Another lightning flash! The Brute gathered his strength, threw Walter off, crawled to his knees, dragged Walter toward him. Walter struggled in vain against the Brute's steely grasp.

"Do something!" I screamed—to whom, I'm not sure. It seemed all was lost.

We were so close to my home. So close. The sound of their fighting faded as Father's ship's bell clanged, louder and louder. This awakened the flute in my pocket, which began playing a shrill, crazed accompaniment to the scene. I looked up and could make out the turrets in the distance, which sizzled and sparked with each flash of lightning. "Please, please . . . ," I whispered, not even knowing exactly what I was asking for.

A constellation of glitter gathered above the roofline of the house. I caught my breath. Held it. The cloud of energy swirled and then coursed across the stormy sky in time to the maniacal tune ripping from Father's flute. In a flash the vapor wrapped itself around the Brute, feet first, snaking up his torso, and finally around his arms and hands.

Paralyzed and shocked, his limbs went rigid and his mouth slack. His eyes, wild with fear, were the only part of him that moved, darting after the cloud of glitter as it encircled his body, rendering him as helpless as a fly encased in spider's silk.

"*She's* doing this!" he screamed. "The witch! Don't you see?"

"Walter, come," said Marni, her eyes never

leaving the Brute. "Get back into the carriage."

Addie sprang into action, lifting Mr. Pugsley, who yelped at her touch. She pulled me, but I didn't move, not until I saw Walter get to his feet. Then Addie and I clambered into the carriage. I swept Annie into my lap, settled Georgie and Mr. Pugsley at my feet, and Addie tended to Mr. Mathers, all of us soaked to the skin and shivering.

The Brute lay there gaping at Marni climbing up to the buggy seat. Walter, incredulous, stared down at his father once more.

"Walter, come," Marni yelled. "Don't look back!"

He climbed up onto the seat and took the reins. "Ya!" he yelled. There was a snap of leather against the mare's hindquarter. With a jerk we were off, barreling down the road, the storm raging around us. The flute still vibrated in my pocket, like panting after great exertion.

I leaned over and peered through the window. The mist had dissipated, and the Brute was struggling to his feet again, stumbling along behind the carriage, a fist raised in the air.

He would never give up. Never. I only hoped that the rain might wash away the wheel tracks or that he'd drop from exhaustion before he reached the house. But something told me that wouldn't happen. Two or three turns in the road were all that separated us from the house.

We pressed on through the storm, hoping against hope that we'd get there in time to somehow stop the series of events that seemed to be hurtling from our grasp, out of control.

19

An ungodly sound rolled in off the water—a kind of hellish howl unlike anything I'd heard before.

It was the sound of the wind—at least that's the only explanation that made any sense whatever. It began as we rounded the final bend toward the house, first as a low rumble, then escalating into a thunderous roar much like the sound of a locomotive. Trees bent back in the face of it, at a most unnatural angle, as if cringing in alarm, or retreating in panic. The wind drove the rain in sharp, slanting sheets and whipped the sea into savage peaks of raging white foam.

By the time Walter slowed the mare to a nervous halt, the sound had risen to a hollow, high-pitched shriek, as though the clouds had burst and the sky itself was screaming. The wind buffeted the carriage, which shook and shuddered against its fury.

"Now, loves, hang on to one another tightly," Addie shouted, "arm in arm! Otherwise I fear we might be swept clear away! I've never heard such a wind—it's like the wrath of God, it is!"

Mr. Mathers shook his head. "I shan't be going in," he hollered. "Poor old Gert is terrified. It's best I get her settled."

"Take her round back," I yelled, "to the garden shed. Until the storm passes!"

The carriage door flew open and was nearly ripped off its hinges. Walter grabbed Addie's arm, and we tumbled out. Curiously, the moon was still visible, casting an eerie light on the flying debris swept up by the wind—garden stakes, twigs and branches, the seat cushions from Mother's wicker settee—all flipping and flying like ghosts in a moonlight dance, gyrating and hurtling to the tune of the wind.

We proceeded together, Marni in the lead; Annie and Georgie in the center, carrying Mr.

Pugsley; Addie, Walter, and I encircling them with a protective chain of hands and arms and elbows. As we moved toward the porch, the wind blew in such a way as to create a sort of safe tunnel for us— as though we were cloaked by the eye of the storm.

We huddled together on the porch. The overhanging roof provided little protection from the rain whipping in almost horizontally. I wriggled from the clutches of our little band, grasped the door latch, and pushed. The door didn't budge, so the six of us pummeled and pounded, demanding to be let inside. My aunt Margaret's face peered through one of the small wavy-glassed windows set along either side of the entrance door. One moment her distorted, fleshy face filled the pane, and next, the dark, swarthy face of my uncle. Our eyes met before his face disappeared. The door remained locked up tight.

I felt a tugging at my hand and looked down to see Annie gesturing frantically toward the path, eyes wide, mouth agape. Barely visible through the driving rain was the Brute, stumbling and crawling, fighting and clawing his way up the path.

"Hurry!" screamed Georgie. "Bang on the door again. We have to get in!"

We pounded and shouted, to no avail. My uncle obviously did not intend to allow us to interrupt his business with the judge. Once the papers were signed, it would be too late. My fate would be sealed.

"I say we break down the door," Walter shouted.

There seemed no other choice. We lifted the long wooden bench that sat opposite the porch rail. Walter held up the front; Addie, the rear; Marni, Georgie, and I, the middle. Annie stood clear.

"One, two, three, *heave*," Walter yelled.

We forged ahead, slamming the end of the bench against the door. It shuddered, but held tight. The Brute was closer now, crawling up the path on hands and knees. Annie whimpered, nervously scanning the distance between her father and the door.

"Annie!" shouted Walter. "Don't pay him any mind. We'll be inside in a moment.

"One, two, three, *heave*!"

This time the crash of wood against wood caused a small splinter in the lower door panel.

"One, two, three, *heave*!"

The lower portion gave way, a ragged rupture out of which spilled light. "One, two, three, *heave*!

"One, two, three, *heave*!

"Heave!"

The bottom of the door shattered. The top panels splintered and slipped haphazardly to the side.

"Come on," Walter commanded. "Careful!"

We dropped the bench and crawled through the gaping hole, avoiding the savage wooden teeth that threatened to bite us.

Aunt Margaret stood on the other side, red-faced, breathing heavily, her hands flying about her jowly face.

"Good Lord, Victor," she shrieked, "come quickly!" She turned toward us, her expression one of fear mixed with anger. "There was no need to break the door down, for heaven's sake!"

She dashed past us and positioned herself in front of the door to the study.

"Victor!" This time it was nothing short of a scream. "They've gone and broken down the door!"

Marni stepped forward and took my aunt by the arm.

"Madam," she said, "you're correct in calling for your husband. This business going on here is not only immoral—I suspect it is illegal as well."

"Get your paws off me!" My aunt's lips were pursed, her eyes wide with fear, or perhaps it was guilt. Her face was beet red. She shook her head rapidly back and forth. Her voice quivered.

"Victor! It's the schoolmistress and she's, she's . . . *threatening* me!" She yanked her chubby arm out of Marni's grasp and inched back toward the library.

"They're in yer father's study," said Addie. "It's where they do their dirty business, isn't it, missus?"

Aunt Margaret didn't answer, just blinked several times, her mouth pulled down in an insolent pout, arms crossed. Addie strode past her. Walter and I followed. "Open up, ye den of thieves!" shouted Addie. Walter pummeled the library door with both fists. Annie and Georgie huddled together, glaring at my aunt from the safety of Marni's shadow. Mr. Pugsley squirmed and growled.

Finally, the library door opened, and there stood my uncle, his black eyes narrowed, boring into me with a look of pure hatred. He turned his stare to Marni.

"Is this the kind of behavior you've been teaching my niece at your school, miss? And who are these scalliwags trespassing on my property?"

"You mean *my* property, don't you, Simmons?"

It was the judge, a sinister smile snaking across his lips, slithering beneath his large, curved mustache.

Marni stepped forward. "We have reason to believe that Miss Lucy's rights are being abused here, that Mr. Simmons forged the letter from his sister-in-law giving up her claim to her rightful inheritance and guardianship of her niece. We also have reason to believe that *you*, sir, have abused your office as a member of the court."

The judge chuckled. "I'm afraid that you, madam, are mistaken. There was a hearing, and I can assure you that Mr. Simmons here has his niece's best interests at heart. Don't you, Victor?"

My uncle smiled. "But of course." He looked at me with barely masked contempt. "You'll be staying on with Miss Maude. Miss Maude, we will provide you with *quite* a hefty allowance for my niece's care." He raised an eyebrow and curled the side of his lip in disgust as his eyes took in her overalls, soaked and caked with mud. "It does seem you could use it to buy yourself something decent to wear."

"My silence about this fraud can't be bought, sir, if that's what you're suggesting," Marni said evenly. "Money means much less to me than justice."

"Is that right?" Uncle Victor snarled. "Well, in that case, we'll just have to find *another* school for her then, won't we? I'm sure there are any number of institutions that would welcome a handsome endowment." He turned his attention back to the judge.

"I believe the matter of payment remains to be dealt with; am I correct?"

The judge held his leather satchel out toward my uncle. "Here it is, just as discussed."

My uncle hesitated, eyeing the satchel hungrily,

a keen glint in his eyes, savoring the moment he'd no doubt been waiting for. At the same time the wind escalated again, and the house itself seemed to tilt and shift, throwing all of us off balance. The storm was fast becoming a hurricane. The house creaked and groaned. The wind screamed around its corners and railed against its walls. As the judge braced himself, the satchel tumbled from his grasp.

Walter, recovering first, dived for the satchel, knocking Aunt Margaret onto her generous behind. She slid along the tilted polished floor like a sledder without a toboggan, screaming all the way. Mr. Pugsley leaped from Annie's arms and took off after Margaret, yapping and nipping at her skirts, which sailed up around her like the billowing sails of a ship, exposing her fat sausage legs and thighs.

A snarl erupted from my uncle's lips as he lunged at Walter. Walter held on tightly to the satchel, stepped aside, and extended his foot. Victor, momentarily stunned and paralyzed with fury, flailed across the floor beside my aunt.

"Hurry, Walter!" shouted Marni, who had pulled Annie and Georgie close. Her eyes had that distant look that told me she was seeing something the rest of us could not see. "Downstairs!" she shouted. "Everyone downstairs!"

Addie and Walter rushed toward the cellarway.

The judge shrugged, an amused expression on his face, and turned toward the front door.

"I trust you will remove these people from my property, Simmons," he said, "and that you yourself will vacate by week's end." He grinned at my uncle, who was scuffling to his feet. The judge ceremoniously turned the knob and pulled open what was left of the door.

"And one more thing," he added. "Be certain you have this door repaired before I move in."

My uncle still seethed with rage, hands shaking, his small eyes darting this way and that, searching for Walter.

"Wait just a minute," he shouted, waving his finger angrily at the judge. "Without that satchel, the sale isn't complete! The boy's gone off with the payment—and you're going to help me recover it!"

The judge laughed. "The satchel is no longer my responsibility. The papers were signed, the title of the property stands in my name, and as far as I'm concerned, the payment was received the moment I was relieved of my satchel. The fact that you allow your household to be overrun by a band of hellions is a problem you'll have to deal with on your own! Or perhaps you could call in the authorities for an investigation!"

He laughed at the unlikelihood of that

occurrence and turned cavalierly on his heel. As he stepped through the doorway, the entire house began to pitch back and forth in the wind, creaking and groaning like an oversized rocking chair. The judge was thrown back inside, and with him the Brute, sprawling and cursing, sliding across the floor as though swimming on dry land! He knocked them all over—the judge, Uncle Victor, and Aunt Margaret, who had barely managed to get back on her feet from her last fall. They toppled this way and that like an odd collection of human bowling pins.

Aunt Margaret screamed, as did Annie. Marni pressed us on toward the cellarway.

"Downstairs, do you hear me?" she repeated. "Lucy, *downstairs*!"

There was something in her eyes and in the steely tone of her voice that frightened me to the center of my being. Suddenly nothing seemed as important as going down to the cellar. I skirted past my stunned aunt sitting propped against the wall, past my uncle embroiled in a scuffle between the Brute and the judge.

The sound of crashing glass in Father's study stopped me in my tracks. I dashed to the doorway, peered inside.

The sea, its huge waves crashing against the side of the house, was pouring in through the window. Though it was impossible—*impossible*—for our house stood far above the high-water mark—the waves crested, the tide swelled and flooded the shoreline, overtaking the house! Water rippled across the floor, streaming over the rug, swirling in angry currents around the legs of Father's desk.

"Lucy! Down to the cellar! *Lucy!*"

Marni's shouts accompanied the next wave that shattered what remained of the beautiful leaded-glass windows. Water surged across the room and about my ankles.

I turned, ran toward Marni, and the two of us fled, hand in hand, toward the cellar door.

It wasn't until we approached the precipice of the cellar stairs that I wondered why in heaven's name we were rushing to *lower* ground as the water was rising.

I passed through the doorway, Marni in front of me on the stairs, pulling me down . . .

down . . .

down . . .

As the water rose, knee deep, I heard a cavernous, haunting aria that could only be one thing: the siren's song. The tone wrapped around me, and my soul surrendered to its call.

I began making my way calmly, deliberately, down the cellar stairs and into the dank darkness below.

20

I stopped on the first landing, my heart racing. I was vaguely aware of all of them at the bottom of the stairs, urging me to continue down into the cellar. Surprisingly, it was only Marni who let me be, searching me with her sea-green eyes, serene and calm in the face of the crisis.

The voices of my aunt and uncle, the judge, and the Brute mingled with the shrieking of the wind to produce a cacophony that raised the hair on the back of my neck. It seemed that the judge, upon seeing the intensity of the storm, and its threat to the house, had decided to retrieve his bag of money.

Once again the house shuddered and bucked. Marni and I were thrown backward against the wall of the stairwell. A crash upstairs on the main floor was immediately followed by a huge sloshing that traveled from the back of the house to the front. The motion of the water rocked the house, top to bottom. The entire structure tilted forward as the tumult rushed along the upstairs hall. Marni and I were tossed, face-first, against the side of the stairwell and, as the wave receded, back again. When the house settled, it leaned precariously backward, the angle of the floor beneath our feet on a great slant.

That was when I realized the house might not withstand the battery of the storm. The others stood below at the foot of the stairs, beckoning with hands and voices. I watched their anguished expressions in a kind of slow-moving, silent dream. Addie and Walter fought their way toward us to pull us to safety, but the floor shook violently, making their ascent impossible.

Water seeped through the ceiling beams, spilling onto my head, back, and legs. Salt stung my eyes. My soaked clothing hung weightily, dragging me down, encumbering my limbs.

The cold embrace of the water and the bizarre rocking of the house transported me back aboard the sloop with Mother and Father. I shut my eyes tightly, but this could not block the memory of the gray water overtaking Father, swallowing up Mother. Still, I followed Marni down. Water surged past us in a vicious cascade. Down to the next step. And the next. I looked back.

Above us in the cellarway was the Brute, clinging to the doorframe. Water splashed about him, holding him captive. His eyes rolled and flashed. He cried out, reaching for me. "Save me! Somebody save me!"

I recoiled. Turned abruptly. Hesitated. The wind and water roared. Below me my friends gestured wildly. So certain did they seem of their safety, so blindly confident in Marni's authority, that I took a step down, then another.

"Help! Help me, for God's sake!"

The Brute reached out with one hand, grasped the doorframe with the other, water crashing around him.

Marni, two steps below me, turned. "Lucy! Give me your hand!"

A collective cry went up as the stairwell began to vibrate. A number of steps tore away. The buckling of the staircase caused a giant rupture, the step separating Marni and me now a gaping hole. Marni was thrown down as the next several steps collapsed like dominoes.

"Jump!" shouted Walter. "Jump! We can catch you!"

I stared into the black space beneath the stairs. The hungry, churning hole would swallow me up.

"Lucy, love, please," Addie shouted, her voice shaking with the vibration of the house. "Miss Marni said we'd be safe here, and I believe 'er! Jump, why don't ye—'tisn't that far! Save yourself, love!"

And still I could not move.

And then, the voice behind me ... "You there ... m-missy! Y-you can help me!" The Brute reached toward me. "I'll get ya down those stairs if ya just lend me a hand! Come *on* now, missy! *Now* I say!"

His eyes shone feverishly. He clenched and unclenched his fist.

Maybe he *could* help me cross the divide. All he'd need was a sturdy yank to pitch him into the stairwell and out of the torrents in the treacherous hallway above.

"Don't risk it, Lucy!" shouted Walter. "He isn't worth it!"

I shook the notion out of my head. Look what had happened to Father trying to help the man, and for what? I inched toward the black hole. Ventured a look down. Perhaps I could clear it.

The house shuddered, tilted even farther back, then forward again. I was nearly lying against the wall of the stairwell, the wall pitched to where the floor had been just moments before.

"Straight to *hell* with the lot of you!" screamed the Brute. "Can't a single *one* of ya help me?" He sputtered, flailed, water crashing past him. "Walter, you good-for-nothing little cuss, what about you? Get your arse up here, boy! That much you owe me!"

"No, Walter," Annie howled. "Don't . . . *please*!" Walter wavered at the edge of the precipice of the stairs, looking desperately between his sister, his father, and me.

A feeling of utter dread came over me. I finally understood Father's terrible dilemma out there on the sloop that day. I forced the voices of my friends and the voice of reason out of my head—in fact, pushed all logical thought aside.

I pulled myself upright and slowly, torturously, dragged myself up to what was left of the perilously tipped staircase, one slippery step at a time. I ignored the insistent cries of my friends. Only Marni remained silent. Her eyes followed me, negotiating each step.

The Brute fought to hang on. His eyes filled with a savage glint. He might panic, overtake me, sending us careening down the hallway and out the door into the torrents outside.

Another wave crashed on the floor above, and a surge of water exploded past, cresting over us. I shook the water from my eyes, shamefully hoping the wave had overtaken him, thus relieving me of my terrible responsibility.

But no, as the water receded I spied him, seven or eight steps up, gasping for air and shaking the water from his mane of wild black hair.

I forced my feet forward, upward, one step, two, a small rest . . . three steps, four, five . . . a deep breath and a prayer . . . six steps. He reached out, and I leaned against the wall, catching my breath. I had no plan other than to anchor myself against the stairwell and grab him. It was not about strength, but faith. He had strength. I willed myself to have faith.

One more step and I could touch him. I could still turn back. No one could fault a person for saving herself, after all.

There was a sudden jolt. A tremendous roar. Screaming upstairs.

I heaved myself up, took hold of his arm.

At that moment glitter began twinkling about my hands, his arms, winding round and round, encircling us like a sparkling cocoon. In the same instant, the massive wave crested, sucking the two of us up into the hall. The colorful mist rendered the Brute immobile and nearly weightless, enabling me to grasp him beneath the chin and tow him through the churning water.

I saw everything in vivid detail—the judge being washed, lifeless, out the front door, the Brute and I carried by the receding wave back along the hallway.

My aunt and uncle fought against the pitch of the floor and the rushing water, struggling toward the window. Uncle Victor slithered ahead like an eel. Behind him my aunt splashed on her hands and knees.

"Grab hold of us!" I shouted. "We need to go down to the cellar!" I finally knew the grim truth: the house would be washed away. But then, at least we could try to swim, couldn't we? It was that or risk being killed when the house collapsed. I reached for Aunt Margaret, but Victor continued to scramble and slide toward the window.

"Victor!" Aunt Margaret screamed, her mouth agape at the sight of the sparkling mist surrounding us. "Lucy says go downstairs! Victor!"

He ignored her, concentrating instead on pulling himself out the window toward his imagined escape.

"Aunt Margaret," I screamed, "take my hand!" She clung to the window frame, gawking at the dazzling aura that held the Brute docile as we bobbed along the hallway canal. She looked frantically between her husband, who already had one foot out the window, and my outstretched palm.

"Victor!" she screamed. *"Victor!"*

He threw his other leg out of the window and perched on the frame, no doubt contemplating the whirlpool below. Once more Aunt Margaret grabbed for him, but he roughly shoved her away. "Let *go* of me, Margaret!" he shouted with an angry spray of spit. "Do you want to drag us *both* down? Better for *one* of us to escape than the two of us drowning!" He licked his thin lips, took a deep breath, pushed her hard with both hands. Without so much as a backward glance, he continued across the windowsill.

Margaret threw herself toward him, grabbed hold of his topcoat. The two of them teetered on the window ledge.

At that very moment the glittering cloud surrounding the Brute and me exploded into a million colors. It spread like wildfire in every direction, along the floors and walls, into every nook and cranny. There was a tinkling sound at first, as the cloud touched the house and was absorbed by it. Gradually, the sound deepened and grew into an earsplitting, creaking noise. From my pocket poured the music of Father's flute, filling the air in a frenzy of sparkling glissandos. It was the sound of transformation, of walls and floors and windows shifting and changing into something very different from what they'd been before. The mist enveloped the velvety papered walls, turning them, from floor to ceiling, into panels of teakwood. The ornate pressed-tin ceilings compressed into sheets of sturdy oak planking. Out front the ship's bell clanged wildly as the house rocked violently forward and back, forward and back, continuing its spectacular conversion.

The back wall of the house glittered and pulsed, stretching itself out into a kind of wedge shape. The window through which my uncle was climbing, my aunt clinging to his back, began to shrink around them. I gaped at the center staircase, glowing and vibrating, straightening itself into a long wooden ladder; the ornately carved post that stood in the center twirled and drilled its way through the floor and on into the cellar.

There was another mighty lurch as the house shifted again. It tipped forward, sending the Brute and me hurtling toward the front door. What used to be the wall had become a slippery slope. Somehow, I managed to maintain my hold on him.

Then another tidal wave. The force ripped the house from its foundation. It heaved and rolled. We slid along the slick surface beneath us, past the cellar doorframe. I caught a glimpse of Marni and the others, flung against the basement walls. All the while the house creaked, and groaned, and piteously sighed.

I instinctively grabbed hold of the door casing and somehow managed to pull the two of us through. The Brute was still groggy and of no help whatever, the sparkling mist rendering him useless and, thankfully, weightless. Miraculously, I was able to plant my feet on something solid and, when I looked about, discovered I was standing on what had been the cellar ceiling.

Marni and the others huddled nearby, gazing upward. My eyes followed those of my loved ones, up, up along the cellar wall.

I gasped.

Above us, the portion of the house that had been thrust from its foundation stood exposed and uncovered like a giant box without a lid, nothing above it but the night sky, the steeply pitched roof beneath the waves. The creaking sound continued as the rain slowed and the bright white moonlight illuminated the scene.

The stone-and-mud cellar walls were fairly glowing, groaning as each stone expanded, mutating into aged timber. The center pole of the hallway staircase sprouted and grew, reaching for the stars. What was left of Mother's elegant dining room curtains swirled up around the center stair post, billowing in the sea air. I rushed to the edge of the wall and looked out over the water below us.

My inverted house bobbed along in the sea, the pitched roof and peak below the water's surface like the keel of a ship. The front of the house, where the porch had been, was curling into an overhanging bow that jutted forward to a sharp point. I peered over the rail of the deck (for that's what the cellar ceiling and walls had become) and gazed at the outer walls. Small strips of pale yellow paint and a bit of gingerbread trim were the last remaining vestiges of my beloved house. The long rectangular windows were shrinking into round portholes, the squared-off corners of the house straightening and softly bulging like the hull of a ship.

What had been the center pole that graced the grand staircase rose majestically from the deck, taking on a new life as the mainmast. The support column holding up the front of the house became the foremast; the column at the rear, the mizzenmast. Her beams running the length of the cellar ceiling, supporting the main floor, were resurrected as yardarms crossing the top of each of the three masts, creating tall T shapes. Each of the yardarms supported a number of crisp white sails. Father's rope ladder he'd hung below my bedroom window now proudly spanned the side of the vessel and the yardarms, inviting us up to the foretop platform for an eagle's-nest view. What used to be the furnace was now a large capstan winch holding the anchor cable. The cable ran along the cathead to the huge anchor from Father's ship, which had graced our side yard since the day, years ago, when Father had left the sea.

I closed my eyes for a moment, attempting to take it all in. My beloved home—my father's "ship on shore," as he loved to call it—had undergone the most amazing transformation. It was still glowing slightly, the shimmer traveling down along the planking and rippling out into the sea. The water took on a calm, phosphorescent quality as the glow dissipated in its depths. The waves subsided, as did the rocking of our vessel. Father' ship's wheel hummed and spun back and forth, begging for the steady guidance of a firm hand.

"Ahhh! Arghhh!"

The strangled cry came from one of the portholes

below the main deck, on what had once been the first floor of my house, but was now probably the berth deck. I looked to the bow to discover Aunt Margaret and Uncle Victor, reaching, reaching out from what used to be the hall window, the mist swirling wildly around them. I gasped as they began a transformation as well, mutating into wood, their flesh stiffening and darkening, becoming etched with knots and lined with grain until all that remained of them was a most remarkable figurehead—their bodies and arms entwined, stretching greedily over the sea, bulging eyes devouring the waves in a desperate, deathly attempt to take hold of something just beyond their grasp.

I stepped back, joining the others, who stood in a tight little circle on the deck, incredulous. All of them, save Marni, seemed rather dazed in the face of the astonishing metamorphosis. Marni waited calmly as, one by one, we stirred, our eyes following the path of ivory moonlight shimmering on the water. A gentle snap roused us further, a sound that has filled many a sailor with delight— the sound of the evening breeze catching and filling the sails.

The Brute began to come to. "Grab him under the arms," Walter yelled.

Addie, Marni, and I each grabbed a limb, and

together we lifted him into the small dinghy that hung alongside the vessel. Walter carefully slipped a large cork life buoy over his shoulders, and Addie positioned a pair of oars securely in the oarlocks. "There," Walter said, satisfied. "No one could say we didn't help him!"

Georgie and Annie stood back, wide-eyed, as Marni and I turned the winch and lowered the dinghy into the sea. "Good-bye, Poppy!" Annie yelled, relief in her voice. It seemed we all understood that he was not to be a part of our voyage, that ensuring his safety had fulfilled any obligation owed him, imagined or otherwise. He slowly awakened, and sat gawking at our magnificent craft sailing into the moonlight. We watched the dinghy drift into the distance as the wind in our sails carried us farther and farther out across the bay.

Marni nodded, a serene smile spreading across her face. "Aye, mates," she said, "it looks like smooth sailing ahead."

21

We crowded together at the bow, quiet in our collective amazement. I rested my head on Addie's shoulder and gathered Annie and Georgie in close. Walter placed a hand on my shoulder, the other on the rail of the ship, his eyes searching out some distant shore. Even Mr. Pugsley seemed content and calm there at our feet, his flat snout raised, sniffing the salt air.

I gazed back to the stretch of shore that had been ours—mine and Father's and Mother's. The garden shed that had previously been dwarfed by the house stood exposed and lonely on the hill.

I wondered, as our ship sailed along, if old Mr. Mathers and Gert had witnessed our passage. Or what people would make of the judge doing the dead man's float across the bay.

I chanced one last look at the now barren and desolate spot where the turrets of our house had graced the horizon, and closed my eyes to memorize the image of what used to be.

Then, as we sailed out toward the open sea, I vowed never to look back again.

It occurred to me that most of our dreams had been fulfilled: Walter was sailing his grand ship, Georgie and Annie would soon have an ocean of safety between them and their father. Addie's fervent desire to have Aunt Margaret and Uncle Victor relinquish control of the house had come to pass, although certainly not in the way she had imagined. Marni, the protector of lost children, had led us all to safety.

And what about me and my dreams?

The house was mine again—perhaps not as I'd ever envisioned it, even in my wildest imaginings, but it was mine. All this and, thanks to Walter, a satchel full of more money than I'd ever laid eyes upon. Of course, there was still Aunt Pru, and the mystery of the Simmons family curse.

We stood together at the helm, each lost in our

own thoughts. What now? What next?

Finally, it was I who spoke.

Never had I felt as sure of something, as decisive as in that moment with the moon illuminating our way. My days of waiting were past. Now was the time to act! "We'll need a crew, and supplies," I said forcefully. "Walter, check the chart room!" I was sure, beyond a doubt, that Father's maps would still be there, waiting, ready to unfurl in our hands. "Gather the maps so we can chart our course!"

Marni nodded. Addie raised her eyebrows and cried, "I say we christen this fine vessel the *Lucy P. Simmons*!" It was all the affirmation I needed.

"Where are we going, Lucy?" Annie asked, her blue eyes wide, trusting.

"To find my aunt Pru," I declared. "Will you help me?" I eyed them, one after the other. "Australia is a long way off, but together we can do it!"

Walter, Georgie and Annie, Addie and Marni gathered around me in a crushing embrace, which I could only take as a solid yes! Mr. Pugsley circled us, yipping at our feet. We joined hands, raised them in the air.

The flute, still snuggled in my pocket, sang as never before; the bell outside the chart room clanged vigorously.

Against a brilliant fireworks display of glittering diamond dust, the *Lucy P. Simmons* carried us off together on what I knew would be a most spectacular voyage.